As if he'd read her mind, a silent but potent sizzle of electricity passed between them.

She stumbled, sure she was about to get up close and personal with the ice, when Grady's arms pulled her to him. She heard the swish of his skates, his legs locked, and she halted against his chest midfall.

"Gotcha," he whispered, his lips near her ear. "Told you I wouldn't let you fall, baby."

And then, magic happened. She lifted her chin to look into his eyes, and a snowflake landed on her cheek. "It's snowing! Look, Grady!"

"I can't," he said, sounding strangely muffled. "Not when you're so beautiful my eyes don't see anything else."

Dear Reader,

There is a magic to Christmas that makes me believe in miracles. Some of this is based in tradition: baking cookies with my kids that I baked with my mother, decorating the tree with ornaments from Christmases past, and even drinking hot chocolate on Christmas Eve with my children.

These traditions filter through the years, combining the past with the present and laying a framework for the future. What I learned, I am teaching my children, and in turn, they will eventually teach theirs. For me, the simple beauty of this is part of what makes Christmas so magical.

What happens when a couple has endured a horrible tragedy just days before Christmas? How do they find the beauty, the magic, in the Christmas season again? More important, how do they find their way back together when every tradition reminds them of what they have lost? These are the questions that propelled me to write *Miracle Under the Mistletoe.*

In this book, you'll meet Grady and Olivia, a husband and wife who are facing their third Christmas without their beloved son. Olivia believes that divorce is the only way to heal, while Grady refuses to give up on the woman he loves. He has a plan to convince her to give their marriage another chance, but even he admits he might need a miracle.

I truly hope you enjoy Grady and Olivia's story and come to love them and the rest of the Foster clan as much as I do.

Happy reading and happy holidays!

Tracy Madison

MIRACLE UNDER THE MISTLETOE

TRACY MADISON

SPECIAL EDITION

Recycling programs
for this product may
not exist in your area.

ISBN-13: 978-0-373-65636-3

MIRACLE UNDER THE MISTLETOE

www.Harlequin.com

Printed in U.S.A.

Books by Tracy Madison

Harlequin Special Edition

Miracle Under the Mistletoe #2154

*The Foster Brothers

TRACY MADISON

lives in Northwestern Ohio with her husband, four children, one bear-size dog, one loving-but-paranoid pooch and a couple of snobby cats. Her house is often hectic, noisy and filled to the brim with laugh-out-loud moments. Many of these incidents fire up her imagination to create the interesting, realistic and intrinsically funny characters that live in her stories. Tracy loves to hear from readers. You can reach her at tracy@tracymadison.com.

To my children: the light of my life.

Chapter One

This is a mistake.

Olivia Markham-Foster knew it the second she entered the dimly lit Italian restaurant. She'd arrived early to get her bearings, and the maître d' had led her to a tucked-away-in-a-corner table that offered plenty of seclusion and privacy. She welcomed the privacy, but the lovey-dovey atmosphere was all wrong. Romance and seduction licked through the air, dripping from the chords of the softly played violin music, twisting her stomach into knots.

Oh, yes. This was most definitely a mistake.

Goose bumps coated her skin and she shivered. She choked down a sip of red wine before placing her finger-entwined hands on her lap. Tonight wasn't about romance or seduction, but Grady… Well, she figured he'd stroll in, take one look at her sitting in this restaurant, at this table, and draw the completely wrong conclusion.

Her husband, for every inch of his tough exterior, was

a romantic through and through, with a soft, melty heart that believed in happily ever after just as fervently as he believed in baseball. Add in the fact that when Grady wanted something, he usually got it, and tonight promised to be more than difficult. He so wasn't going to like what she had to say.

But Olivia had made a decision and, come hell or high water, she was going to proceed as planned—even if she felt ridiculous for bringing him to a swanky restaurant for an intimate dinner. Maybe the location was Samantha's fault, but it was too late to change that. Now, she had to follow through. Her life depended on it. If she was being honest, Grady's life depended on it, too. Continuing on this way, stuck in place at opposite ends, was hurting both of them.

Olivia sighed and fiddled with her wineglass. He wouldn't see it that way, though. He'd toss the same arguments at her that he always did, remind her of what they'd once been—as if she could possibly forget—and try to cloud her decision so she'd back down.

"Not this time," she whispered. This time, she would stay strong.

Without warning, her throat tightened and telltale tingles sped along her arms. Whatever composure she'd managed to cling to evaporated in a rush of recognition. *He* was here. She didn't need to look up to know that. Her body sensed Grady. Hell, her soul sensed him. It had been that way from the very beginning. She looked up anyway.

And that was another mistake.

She blinked, tried to force herself to look beyond him, but that proved impossible. Grady Foster didn't simply walk into a room. His long-legged gait held equal amounts of danger and grace—like a panther, wild and untamed. Blacker-than-coal hair framed a sculpted, almost chiseled face, ending just above the hard angle of his jaw, pulling attention to the high-planed lines of his cheeks.

His gaze met hers. The distance between them didn't mask the glitter of recognition, anticipation, in his cinnamon-speckled eyes. Her heart rippled like a caged butterfly, its wings beating mercilessly against her breastbone, begging for release—for freedom. Again, the image of a panther, catching sight of its prey and moving in for the kill, winged into her mind.

And she *was* Grady's prey.

Okay, not fair. He didn't want to cause her harm. Just the opposite, actually. He wanted to pull her into his arms and give her the world. He wanted them to reclaim the life they'd lost, but that—like so many other things—was impossible.

He approached in ground-swallowing steps, every part of him focused on her. She stole another quick sip of wine before pulling in a breath, before relaxing her muscles and giving him the cool, practiced smile she'd perfected over the past three years. If she kept her emotions hidden and her voice calm and sure, she'd get through this. Somehow.

Just as she had everything else.

He slung his long, sinewy frame into the chair across from her and nodded. He tugged at his tie, loosening it ever so slightly. If she wasn't fighting so hard to remain in control, she might feel ashamed for bringing him to a place that required a suit. Grady hated wearing them. A pity, really. Very few men looked quite as sexy as her husband did in a well-fitted suit.

"Thank you for agreeing to meet," she said in a soft, clear voice. Her hope was to take control of the conversation, of this meeting, before they lapsed into the murky footsteps of their past. She also wanted to hide how much his presence shook her. "I wasn't sure if you would."

Disbelief creased his forehead with lines. "You're my wife, Olly. Why would you think I'd refuse to see you? I've been waiting for this…waiting for you to reach out… for a long time."

"But I'm not—" She coughed to clear her throat. He was right. Regardless of how often she'd turned away from his attempts at reconciliation, she knew he'd show. He hadn't given up hope. But she had, so she stuck with the lie. "I wasn't sure," she repeated.

"Then you haven't been paying attention." The brown in his eyes darkened, and his jaw clenched tight. "I'm available whenever you need me. I've made that clear to you, haven't I?"

"Y-you have, but… Well—" She broke off when she saw the waiter approaching their table. Relief that she had a few precious minutes to regain her equilibrium saturated in, easing the acid roiling in her stomach.

The waiter set menus in front of them, gave a quick rundown of the evening's specials, and took Grady's drink order before leaving them alone again.

Grady returned his thickly lashed gaze to hers. "Let's start over. I'm glad you called, Olivia. I'm glad we're here together. We haven't been to a place like this since before—" Rubbing his hand over his jaw, he frowned. "In years," he said, correcting his near error.

It was so very hard not to react to the words he almost said. A shot of familiar sadness swept in, nearly crippling her. If she gave in to the sadness, she'd break down. The guilt would come next and before she knew it, she'd be up to her eyebrows in emotional quicksand. So she did what she always did—she shoved her feelings away as hard and as fast as she could. "Yes. Years. And this is a nice restaurant, but Grady…"

A few seconds passed while he waited for her to finish

speaking, but when it became clear that she wasn't going to, he raised his shoulders in question. "But what?"

Now or later? Dinner first would be best. Especially if they could manage cordial conversation. She gave her head a quick shake. "Nothing. Never mind."

"I know you better than that, Olly. I'm here and I'm not going to bite. So tell me…but what?"

"Fine. Here goes." Olivia inhaled a quick breath in an attempt to steady herself. "I know you're probably thinking that I brought you here to…to…"

He sighed in exasperation. "Okay, Olivia. What's going on? I think you asked me to meet you here for what? A good meal?" His voice held a teasing quality, but the lines in his forehead deepened even more. "Please tell me what I'm thinking."

Oh, God. Why had she listened to Samantha? Coming here for this conversation had been her idea, and Olivia should have known better. "That I want us to get back together, and that I brought you here to discuss reconciliation."

His entire body stilled as he appraised her.

For not the first time in her adult life, Olivia wished she had the ability to sit as still and quiet as he. To let him grow uncomfortable enough that he'd fill the silence. But he was the panther, not she. "I don't—want to get back together, that is. I thought we could talk. We need to talk. But not about reconciliation."

A new round of disbelief hardened his expression and glinted in his eyes. "I put on a suit, drove across town and met you in a romantic restaurant so you could inform me that nothing has changed? We could have had this conversation on the phone, or at the house, or— Hell, Olly, what were you thinking?"

"I wasn't thinking…I didn't know— Samantha recommended this restaurant. She said the atmosphere was conducive to a private discussion. This conversation shouldn't happen over the phone, and you haven't lived in the house for months—close to a year, actually—so I was afraid you'd feel like we were on my turf." *Calm down,* she instructed herself. *Don't get rattled.* Straightening her posture, she said quietly, "I thought a place neither of us had ever been would even the playing field. So to speak."

The tight, hard way he held his mouth relaxed. "Samantha told you to bring me here?"

"Yes. But I didn't know—" Olivia narrowed her eyes at the devilish smirk on Grady's face. Samantha Hagen was *her* best friend, but she was a huge fan of Grady's. She wanted Olivia and Grady to reconcile almost as much as Grady did. "This isn't funny! I'm trying to explain."

Rather than disappearing, or even easing, the smirk widened. "I've always liked Sammy. I haven't talked to her in ages. How's she doing?"

"She's fine," Olivia snapped, annoyed with the change in his demeanor. "You could even say that business is booming." Samantha earned her living as a divorce attorney. "In fact, she's busier than ever."

His smirk vanished. "I'm happy for her, but—"

"You don't believe in divorce," she said, finishing his sentence.

"That isn't entirely true. I don't believe in backing away from a commitment until all other alternatives have been exhausted." He gave her a piercing look. "You used to feel the same."

A slew of tremors skidded down her spine, but she kept her voice steady. "I used to feel a lot of ways that I no longer do. Things change."

Before she could blink, his hand captured hers. His touch, as simple as it was, wove into her and sparked a touch of desire deep in her belly. Dear God, she'd missed his touch. She pulled out of his grasp and flexed her fingers. "Things change," she said again.

"*That* hasn't changed. You still want me. As much as I want you. Why do you fight against us so hard?"

"Because physical attraction isn't enough."

"You keep saying that, but—" The waiter appeared, delivering Grady's beer, and asked for their orders.

Olivia had barely glanced at the menu. She started to say that they'd need a few more minutes when Grady stepped in and ordered for both of them. He'd ordered for her on plenty of occasions in the past, a trait she used to find endearing, but this time it riled her up. More than necessary, but she couldn't stop her frustration from fueling into anger.

When the waiter left, she glowered at her husband. "Maybe I wanted something instead of chicken marsala. Maybe I thought the scallop linguine sounded good."

He raised his left eyebrow. "Really? But you love chicken marsala."

"That's not the point."

"Then what *is* the point?"

An exasperated huff pushed out of her lungs. "You could've asked."

"Why would I?"

"Why wouldn't you?"

"Because you've always ordered chicken marsala at every Italian restaurant we've ever gone to." He shook his head in confusion. "Why would I think that had changed?"

"Why would you think it hadn't? I'm not the same woman you married. Many, many things have changed. Why can't you accept that?"

"If you want linguine, I'll get you linguine." He started

to raise his hand to gesture for the waiter, but she grabbed his arm and tugged.

"Stop! Please, Grady. You can't fix everything! You can't make everything right." She gulped a mouthful of air. "Quit trying."

He muttered a curse. "I apologize for ordering for you. It's an old habit, and I did it without thinking. My intent wasn't to upset you."

Heavy tears pressed against her eyes. One blink and they'd come pouring out. She couldn't—wouldn't—cry in front of Grady. If she did, he would doubt her decision. And if he pushed her too hard, she'd probably capitulate and spend the next year, two, or possibly the rest of her life in the same empty place she'd already spent far too long. No way could she let that happen.

It was time. She needed to say what she came here to say before her emotions got the best of her. Waiting until after they ate now seemed absurd and pointless. She tried to talk, but the words got stuck in her throat.

Unsaid emotions drenched the air between them. Grady stared at her, his lips taut and his eyes hooded. Comprehension filtered over him. He expelled a harsh-sounding breath. "This isn't about the chicken, is it?"

"No. It isn't."

"What is this about then, Olivia?"

She almost couldn't say the words. Memories of their past—of how happy their lives had been—whispered through her mind. She opened her mouth but closed it just as fast.

"Well?" He sounded resigned, as if he knew what was coming and just wanted to get it over with. "It's me. You can tell me anything."

Raising her chin, she met his gaze with hers, and that was all it took to put her back on course. No matter how good those early memories were, they weren't enough. "I want a divorce," she said softly but with conviction.

His shoulders stiffened as he took in her statement. "What did you say?"

"I said that I want a divorce." Her heart pounded so fast and so hard that her chest almost hurt from the pressure. "I'm sorry, Grady. It's time. You know it's time."

"I know nothing of the sort." Grady's eyes narrowed. "I'm not interested in a divorce. And we have a long way to go before I'll even consider it."

"How much longer? We haven't been a real couple for two—almost three—years."

"We were together and happy for seven."

"That was a lifetime ago."

"*Our* lifetime, Olly. Yours and mine. Why won't you give us a chance?" Frustration colored his tone and a gleam of hurt pooled in his eyes. "What are you so afraid of?"

"I'm not afraid. But you moved out of the house nine months ago. We lead separate lives. There isn't any reason to pretend any longer, Grady." She lifted her chin. "Our marriage is over."

"I moved out because you asked me to. I've kept to our agreement of one phone call a week. I don't drop by without your permission." He combed his fingers through his hair in a quick, jagged movement. "And do you know why I've done these things?"

She knew. Of course, she knew. "Because I asked you to. Because you hoped that a little distance would bring us closer together. But that hasn't happened."

"Because you haven't let it."

One deep breath in, another out, and she said, "We're at the end. You have to know that."

He shook his head in disbelief. "I don't know that. What

I know is that we are *not* finished. What I know is that there is still plenty between us. Tell me I'm wrong."

The pain in her chest expanded. "You're not wrong," she said in a shaky whisper. "There are feelings here. There will probably always be feelings between us, but we can't—"

"What?" he demanded. "We can't *what?*"

"Recover. Be the same as we were. Turn back time." But dear God, she wished they could. She swallowed a sob. "We can't fix the one thing that needs to be fixed."

Every hard edge softened. He closed his eyes and drew in a long breath that must have reached his toes. When he opened his eyes again, she no longer saw frustration. She saw compassion, as well as the same raw pain that met her gaze every time she looked into a mirror. *This* was what they shared now: pain and loss. And how were they to build anything meaningful, anything positive, with that as their foundation?

"You're right. I would do anything—give up anything—to change what happened. But I can't, sweetheart. You can't, either. But we—you and I—can forge something new, something different. It will never be the same, but we *can* be happy again. I believe that, Olly. If you'll just give us a real chance." His jaw set in that stubborn line. "Unless... Is there someone else?"

"No," she said instantly. "But there never will be for either of us if we're still married to each other."

"I don't want anyone else," he said in a growl.

"Fine! Maybe I do! M-maybe I'm ready to start dating again." The lie fell easily from her lips, but not so easily from her heart. "Maybe *I'm* ready to move on."

"Then move on with me."

He made it sound so easy. As if simply saying yes would magically set everything right. And she—God help her—wanted to say yes. But she'd had more peace in the past nine months than she'd had before he moved out. That made her answer clear and absolute. "I can't. There is nowhere left for us to go. It's been three years since we've been happy, Grady."

"Yup," he said, surprising her with his agreement. "But in those three years, have we seen a counselor? Have we had an honest conversation about what happened?" He shook his head. "No, we haven't. Therefore, all alternatives have not been exhausted."

"Tell me the past nine months haven't been a relief?" she countered.

"They've been hell," he said quietly.

"Not for me." This wasn't the entire truth. She'd missed her husband. At times, had even ached to see him, to hear his voice, to feel his arms close around her at night. But the greater part of her had found relief. Amnesty. A reprieve from the darkness. "I—I don't need your agreement to file for divorce."

"No. You don't. Oregon is a no-fault state. But that doesn't mean I won't put up a fight."

"It would be easier if you would agree. I would like it so much better if we were on the same page. I don't want to fight you," she admitted in a rush of syllables. "But I can't stand still anymore. Please understand."

"Understand what? That you're my wife? I love you, Olivia. Doesn't that mean anything to you now?"

And she still loved him. She probably always would. But sometimes, love wasn't enough. It sucked, and she hated it, but that was the way life worked. "No, Grady. It doesn't." She cringed at her tone—at another lie—but backing down wasn't an option. "I need this. I need to move on, and I can't do that until we are officially over with."

Defeat, followed by a hot blaze of emotion ripped over Grady's features. "What would Cody say to this? Have you thought about that?"

His words slammed into her, shaking her bravado and stealing her breath away. "Don't you do that. Don't you bring Cody into this."

"Oh, come on, Olivia. Let's be honest with each other about this for once." Grady clenched his hands into fists. "This is completely about Cody. This has everything to do with Cody. So let me ask you again—what would *our son* have to say about this?"

Every iota of calmness she'd managed to maintain evaporated. This was too much. She needed to get away from here—from him. Standing from the table, she grabbed her purse and set an icy glare upon her husband. "I'm going to have Samantha start the paperwork. You might want to consider hiring an attorney."

With that, she left the restaurant in slow, measured steps that belied her off-the-charts emotional state. Her entire body quaked as sadness mixed with shock and anger rushed through her. How dare he? Bringing their son into this was wrong.

She made it to her car without shedding a tear. Knowing Grady was apt to come looking for her, to make sure she was all right and to offer her comfort, she drove down the street a few miles before pulling into another parking lot, this one in front of a grocery store.

Crossing her arms over the steering wheel, she allowed herself a good, shoulder-shaking cry. God, she missed Grady. But she missed her little boy more. Missed every little thing about him. And that was one reason being around Grady was so difficult. Cody had been the spitting image of his daddy. So when Grady smiled, she saw Cody's smile. When she looked into Grady's eyes, she saw her son's eyes. Even their laughs were the same. The resemblance between father and son kicked her in the gut every time she laid eyes on Grady.

It didn't matter that the love she felt for her husband was as real today as it was on the day they married. It didn't matter how often she woke in the middle of the night and reached for him, only to find herself alone. And it didn't matter that her entire life felt emptier without him. Because as bad as all those things were, they didn't compare to losing her child.

Grady thought she blamed him for the death of their son. Nothing could be further from the truth, not that he believed her. It would be easier if she did blame Grady, she admitted. She'd be able to forgive him. Forgiving herself, though, seemed impossible.

It was *her* fault that her husband and son were in the wrong place at the wrong time. It was *her* fault that they were driving on ice-slicked roads instead of where they should have been: safe and sound at home. She was the one who put off taking Cody to see Santa for weeks, and she was the one who put the bug in Cody's ear about Daddy taking him to see Santa instead. And when Grady came to her and suggested they go together, as a family, she'd pushed the whole father-and-son-outing idea until he agreed.

Her selfish want to have a few hours to herself, to relax from all of the shopping, wrapping, baking and decorating had resulted in the loss of everything that meant anything.

So no, she couldn't be with Grady. It was too hard. He brought too many memories, too many emotions, to the surface for her to find any type of peace.

Forty-five minutes later, Grady strode through the cemetery, not stopping until he reached his son's gravestone.

Nearly three years since he'd heard Cody's laugh, since he'd seen the boy's brown eyes light up in humor, since his arms had held his child to his chest in a hug. How was that possible? The pain ignited inside as if the loss had occurred yesterday.

Usually, Grady could set the hollow ache aside and move forward, do whatever needed to be done, and portray a man who lived and breathed and loved. It was only during these moments—when he came to visit Cody's resting place—that he gave up the charade. There was no reason to pretend here. Not when it was just them.

He shivered, partly from the memories and partly from the dusting of snow that had fallen earlier all throughout the city. It seemed every recent winter brought more snow than the residents of Portland, Oregon, were accustomed to, but this was the earliest snowfall that Grady could recall. Silly and sentimental, maybe, but it was almost as if Cody were reaching out to him. His son had loved everything about winter.

Bending at the knees, Grady brushed the light layer of snow covering the etched letters that spelled out his son's name. Losing Cody wasn't right. It wasn't fair, either. But hell, what in life was fair? Things happened. Some of the things were good, some of them were bad, and some of them were so bad that you didn't think you'd ever recover. Grady almost hadn't. But you played the hand you were dealt. You found a way to get through, to get a grip, and you carried on.

Not that carrying on without his son had been an easy task. Far from it. Never had he experienced such a profound loss, and he prayed to whatever God existed that he would never face anything so excruciating again.

"Hey, kiddo. I've been thinking a lot about you today. Every day, really. You're never far from my thoughts."

Grady's throat seemed to shrink as he spoke, but he continued to talk, knowing from past experience that as hard as these visits were, they also helped him feel close to Cody. "I saw your mom tonight. You should've seen her, son. She looked beautiful."

Olivia had worn her dark brown hair loose and long, framing her face, showing off her gorgeous wide-set blue eyes. The second he saw her, he was lost all over again. God, what a fool he was. When Olivia had asked him to dinner, he'd been sure that tonight would be the night he'd been waiting for: the night they'd finally begin to clear the air and move toward reconciliation.

"I don't want to give up on her," Grady murmured into the cold night air. "I promise I'll keep trying, Cody. Though, I'll have to give her a few days to calm down. I upset her tonight, son. I didn't mean to."

When Olivia had left Grady alone at the restaurant, it was all he could do not to jump up and follow. He hated not knowing if she was okay. He hated knowing that there were some things he couldn't shield her from. But he forced himself to stay put. He'd dealt her a low blow by bringing Cody into the conversation. He probably shouldn't have, but he yearned to talk to Olivia about Cody, to revel in the life of their son together. But the facts were plain. She wasn't ready. After tonight, he wondered if she ever would be.

He'd believed that given enough distance—since that seemed to be what Olivia needed—they'd find their way together again. So he'd held his tongue, waited for her to come to him, to say all the words she never had, and hoped that once that happened, they might have a chance at repairing their marriage. But now she'd asked for a divorce. Something that she'd hinted at often enough but had never before said straight-out.

"I wish..." Grady swallowed the rest of his statement away. He'd like to turn back time, just as Olivia had said, and return to that snowy, blustery day nearly three years earlier. With Christmas only two days away, five-year-old Cody had wanted to visit Santa before the big day. To be honest, Grady hadn't been in the mood for a trip to the mall. Dealing with mobs of people didn't sound nearly as much fun as playing in the snow with his son.

But Cody had looked at him with those big, brown eyes and pleaded in the way that only a five-year-old can. So off they went on a father-and-son outing. Grady would never, for as long as he lived, forget the look of pure joy on Cody's face when he sat on Santa's knee. That smile made the crowded mall, the long lines and the grumpy shoppers worthwhile.

The snow was falling fast and furious when they left, and Grady had a minute—one freaking minute—where he considered hanging out in the food court to give the storm a little more time to work its way through. But he'd worried that it would get worse with night approaching, so he made the decision to get them home. Where it was safe. Where Olivia waited.

So yes, he'd give anything and everything to revisit that day and spend the hours building snowmen with his son instead of going to the mall. Or left an hour earlier— later—hell, fifteen minutes in either direction might have made the world of a difference, might have put his car somewhere other than in the path of a driver who'd consumed far too many drinks.

"Stop. It's done. Nothing to do about that now." True, that. But knowing something couldn't be changed didn't stop a man from wishing it could. He brushed his fingers over his son's name again, recalling the joy their lives had been together. They were, in nearly all ways, the perfect family. Or, at least, the way a family should be.

Yep, he'd had it all. The American dream. And now…

"Your mom blames me, Cody. She swears that she doesn't, but I know she does. If she'd just scream at me and quit trying to shield both of us from her feelings, we might stand a chance."

Grady even understood why Olivia felt the way she did. He'd likely have had the same demons to fight if their roles were reversed, if Olivia had been at the wheel that day. He understood her blame completely. Hell, he'd yet to stop blaming himself.

Olivia stood motionless, her eyes glued to the scene in front of her. She wasn't close enough to hear Grady's words, but the sight of him kneeling at their son's gravesite softened everything inside. They hadn't been here together since that horrible, exhausting day they buried their son.

She swallowed, trying to ease the pressure in her chest, trying to find a way to feel normal. Even if only for a second. A choked-sounding sob escaped. She barely remembered what normal was. The tenor of Grady's voice whisked along the November wind, wrapping around her, bringing a strange sort of anonymous comfort.

How odd that being with him brought her pain, but this—just listening to his voice—eased the panicky, twisty feeling that had existed within her for so long. The safety of distance, perhaps. Or the simple fact that he didn't know she lurked nearby. Or maybe because she'd finally, after all of this time, made a decision about their marriage.

None of that mattered at the moment, because all she wanted was to feel normal again. So she didn't think. She didn't give herself a second to consider the ramifications, to wonder if she should or if she shouldn't. She just stepped forward, her eyes resting on the one man—the only man—she'd ever loved. Her shoes crunched in the snow, the sound echoing in the silent night like tiny bursts of fireworks, but Grady didn't turn his head.

She kept moving forward, expecting him to hear her, expecting him to stop talking and face her, at any minute. He didn't. She stopped a few feet from where he knelt, close enough to make out his words, close enough to recognize the husky, emotional quality in her husband's voice.

"It's almost Christmas again, son. Soon, people will be putting up their Christmas trees, decorating their houses with lights. Kids will visit Santa." Grady's tone deepened. "I try not to be envious. I try not to think about what we would be doing if you were still with us. But it's hard."

Oh, God. No. She didn't want to hear this. No, no, no. She took one silent step backward, and then another. But Grady kept talking, each syllable slicing into her like a blade.

"I saw this train set the other day, and I immediately thought how much you would love it. I had the box in my hands before I remembered...before I realized—"

She blinked and one tear, and then another, fell. How often had the same thing happened to her? Too often. "Stop," she whispered. "Please stop."

Grady rose to his feet lightning-fast. His arms crushed around her and his mouth pressed against the top of her head. "I didn't know you were here. I'm sorry, Olly. I'm so sorry you heard...."

She burrowed her head into his chest, knowing she should pull away but unable to find the strength to do so. His arms felt so good around her. She closed her eyes and breathed in his familiar scent, allowing herself a few minutes of comfort.

He tightened his hold and kissed her hair softly. Gently. She sighed and nestled in deeper, wanting more, wanting everything she'd lost, wanting to be—even if only for one more night—normal. Again, the thought that she should pull back—leave and go home—processed, but her body refused to listen. So she hung on, curled her fingers into the back of Grady's coat and tugged him closer.

The twisting sensation in her stomach gave way to warmth. Tendrils of heat teased through her muscles, winding through her body like a vine. Grady's hands pressed against her back, offering her comfort, reminding her of everything they'd once been, of the passion they'd once shared, of the life they'd once had. It was a lot. It was too much to take in, too much to handle with her raw emotions, so she forced her arms to drop and her legs to retreat.

"I'm sorry I interrupted you," she mumbled. "I should leave."

"No, you shouldn't." He held out a hand. "Come here, Olly. Let me hold you."

Her logical brain insisted she needed to hightail it out of there, but her body moved forward. She placed her hand in his, and he pulled her toward him. She looked up into Grady's eyes, and before she knew what was happening, his lips were on hers.

And everything else disappeared.

Chapter Two

Olivia rolled over in bed and stretched. She reached blindly for Jasper, but instead of the soft, warm fur of her cat, her palm slapped against an empty pillow. Normally, the oversize Siamese perched himself next to her head, anxiously waiting for her to wake up. The second she'd open her eyes, the hungry meows would begin.

Weird. She couldn't remember one morning in the last—

Oh, no! She hadn't. Had she? Her skin warmed when the prior night's events invaded her memory. Oh, yes. God help her, yes she had. Grady had kissed her. She'd kissed him back, and then followed him here, to his apartment. More kissing ensued. There were a few glasses of wine in there somewhere, along with the food Grady had brought home from the restaurant, and then more kissing. Her fingers touched her lips. A lot of kissing. A lot of touching.

Oh, hell. A lot of everything.

Fire had roared through her blood, she'd wanted him so badly. Still wanted him, if her body's current reaction was anything to go by.

And how stupid was that? Panic threaded in when she peeked through half-opened eyes, expecting to find Grady watching her. When she didn't see her husband anywhere, she opened her eyes fully and sat up, pulling the blankets around her, taking stock.

The room was simple and basic, containing only a bed, a dresser, one nightstand and a lamp. Other than a few pictures of Cody and one of her, the room was bare of any decorative embellishments. She remembered that the rest of the apartment was the same: functional, but without any of the extras that created a home. Not so much a bachelor pad as a place to get by, one day at a time, until something better came along.

And knowing her husband the way she did, that meant waiting for *her*. Waiting for the day that he could move back into their home to take up where they'd left off.

Olivia brought her knees tight to her chest and wrapped her arms around them in an effort to find her balance. This was bad. Monumentally bad, even. She heard movement from beyond the bedroom, along with a cacophony of banging and clanking. Grady was in the kitchen, probably making her breakfast. Her husband's humming hit her ears next. *Humming!*

She groaned. Now what? She'd finally found the strength to ask for a divorce, and then she'd followed up with a roll in the hay? What kind of a woman did that—and enjoyed it, no less? Okay, huge understatement. She'd more than enjoyed it. She'd basked in their lovemaking. Images of him touching her, of her touching him, rushed in. Red-hot heat licked into her limbs. Last night wasn't

Grady's fault. She'd wanted him as much as he'd wanted her. Physically, anyway. And for what? To feel normal?

The humming in the next room changed to whistling. She tried to relax, but her muscles bunched into tighter knots. Her eyes drifted to a photo of Cody and another round of panic hit her squarely in her chest. What had she been thinking? Stupid question. She hadn't thought. No, what she had done was react—to Grady's voice, his touches…his kisses.

"Calm down," Olivia murmured. "Think this through."

Squeezing her eyes shut, she allowed herself a moment to relive their lovemaking. Warmth and tenderness exploded inside as the memories wove through her. Dear God, she'd missed him. Last night was like coming home. "This is good," she whispered. "Keep going."

She envisioned walking into the kitchen and laying a kiss on her husband, on the image of his arms circling her and holding her tight, of her telling him that she wanted to move forward. Or, at least, try to move forward. A slow buzz trickled over her, further easing the weight on her shoulders. Maybe last night hadn't been a mistake, but rather, a twist of fate to stop her from divorcing Grady. Was that possible?

Maybe. If she were to believe in signs, then this— having sex with her husband the night she'd asked for a divorce—was a huge one. Opening her eyes, she breathed in deeply and let the idea simmer. The panicky feeling was still there, but for maybe the first time in years, a tiny speck of hope existed. Why? What had changed? Maybe…maybe she'd needed nothing more than to take a step toward Grady, instead of pushing him away?

Her gaze found Cody's picture again. Her beautiful boy's face, forever captured in a photograph, made her heart flutter in a saccharine-sweet reminder. His mischievous smile and the light in his eyes turned the flutter into a stabbing sensation. Cody was still gone. A fresh wave of agony pulled a sob from her throat. How could she feel happy, even for a minute, without him? She couldn't. So, no. Nothing had changed.

The walls closed in and suffocating pressure enveloped her. Last night, no matter how wondrous, was a mistake. Now she had to explain that to Grady. But first, she had to get out of his bed and put some clothes on. Sitting here naked while he cooked her breakfast wasn't the way to fix anything.

That thought galvanized her into action. She scrambled off the bed and grabbed her clothes. Bra…check. Panties… check. She slipped her dress on over her head. The whistling from the next room grew louder…closer.

Crap! Where were her shoes? She scanned the floor and then dropped to her knees and peered under the bed. No shoes. *Think, Olivia! Where did you leave them?*

The door opened while she still had half of her body stuck under the bed. She jumped and hit her head on the bed frame. A curse that would redden a sailor's cheeks flew from her lips.

"Checking for monsters?" Grady's warm tenor was filled with forced humor. "Or just seeing what I store under my bed?"

"Neither." She rubbed the back of her head while pulling herself upright. "I…um…was trying to find my shoes."

"In the living room." He gave her a quick once-over. "Are you okay?"

Olivia nodded, struck speechless by the sight of her husband. He stood by the door in navy flannel pajama bottoms and a black T-shirt that fit him like a second skin. She had a moment's relief that he even wore a shirt, but that didn't dispel the need swirling inside.

The tray in his hands held plates with bacon and eggs, along with a couple of mugs filled with coffee. "You… didn't have to make me breakfast," she said.

"I wanted to," he said simply. "I figured you'd be ravenous after—"

"Right. Well…um…thank you, but I'm actually not h-hungry." Her stomach growled, belying her words. Damn him for knowing her so well, anyway. "I'm not *that* hungry," she corrected. "And I should probably be getting home. For Jasper."

"Jasper will be fine for a little longer." Grady nodded toward the tray. "I had this grand idea of breakfast in bed, but now that you're up, we might as well eat in the kitchen." Before leaving the room, he tossed her one of his sexy-as-sin grins. "Come on. Before everything gets cold."

She eyed the door he stepped through and considered her options. She wanted—needed—to leave and go home where she felt safe. Where she could be alone and think about everything that had gone on here, and then—after she felt whatever she was going to feel—she could tuck it all away and work on forgetting. As if none of it had ever happened.

Yes. That was the plan she wanted to proceed with. But jeez, he'd made her breakfast! How in the world was she supposed to ignore that? She tried to imagine strolling out of the bedroom, finding her shoes, telling Grady, "Thanks, but no thanks," while he sat at his kitchen table with food he'd prepared for her.

A sigh slipped out. She couldn't do that. He deserved so much more than that. Okay, then, they'd eat. She could give him that much. But somehow, before she left this apartment, she'd have to dig deep and find the strength to tell him that last night hadn't altered her decision.

"Olly? You okay in there?" Grady called out. "Should I bring the tray back in?"

"No! I'm coming." As bad as this was, eating in the bedroom would be ten times worse. Straightening her spine, she plastered a smile on and exited the room. Her stomach growled again when she sat down at his minuscule kitchen table, a reminder that Grady knew her far better than she knew herself. And for whatever reason, that annoyed her.

"Hi," she said. "I...I was looking for a hairbrush."

"Hi, yourself. The brush is in the bathroom, but you don't need it. I like the mussed morning-after look on you." He gave her a closer look. "Actually, you're a little pale. How hard did you hit your head?"

"I'm okay. A bit of a headache, maybe." Just that fast, her annoyance fled. It wasn't his fault that he knew her so well, and his concern touched her. It also made her feel like a heel. He was still watching her, so she said, "And I think I'm hungrier than I realized."

"Dig in. I'm going to grab you something for that headache." He reached over and tucked a strand of her hair behind her ear. "We'll have you feeling better in no time."

She nodded and tried to focus on her meal. Even though he'd cooked everything just as she liked it—the bacon was crisp without falling apart, the coffee was strong and hot and the scrambled eggs had the exact right amount of cheddar cheese melted on top—it all tasted flat. She might as well have been eating cardboard.

Grady returned and handed her a couple of capsules. "Ibuprofen. You don't have a lump, do you?"

She swallowed the pills with a gulp of coffee. "Lump?"

"On your head. From hitting it?" He took the chair across from her. "Do you need some ice?"

"Oh!" She reached up and felt the back of her head. "Nope. No lump."

An odd expression darted over his face, but he nodded. "Good."

The next several minutes were filled with silence as they ate. She managed to clear about a third of her plate before giving up the pretense. With a sigh, she pushed her plate back and picked up her coffee. "Thanks again. This was really good."

He eyed her doubtfully. "You're welcome. You didn't eat that much, and I think that's the third time you've thanked me this morning. Are you sure you're okay?"

"I'm feeling much better." *Liar!* her mind screamed. "But Grady, I need to tell you...I mean to say..." Setting her cup down, she twisted her fingers together. "We should probably talk—"

He gave her a long, searching look. "I know you're uncomfortable about last night, but there isn't any reason to put it under a magnifying glass." He pushed a lock of black hair off of his forehead. "We don't have to talk about last night, Olly. I'm just glad you're here."

"We don't?" Her mind zeroed in to the first part of his statement and a good amount of tension evaporated. Oh, thank God for small favors. Maybe last night had been nothing more than goodbye sex. A last hurrah of sorts. She could live with that—couldn't she? "Well, good. I—I guess I should get home to Jasper."

She started to push back from the table, knowing she should say more, knowing she should clarify that his statement meant what she thought it meant, but not sure how to get it out without sounding like an idiot, when Grady said, "Don't leave. Please? I want to spend the day with you." His husky tone poured into her like a salve. God, she loved his voice. "I was thinking we could get an early start on Christmas shopping. Maybe even—"

"It isn't even Thanksgiving yet. I haven't thought about buying gifts." And she certainly hadn't considered shopping with Grady. The last time they'd gone Christmas shopping together was forever ago. Before... Well, just *before*. "I don't know. It probably isn't a good idea."

"Well," he said slowly, his gaze level with hers. "I...I have an idea. Something I would like to share with you, but I'm not sure how you'll respond."

Warning signals bleeped in her brain. "Respond to what?"

"I thought we could shop for Cody...for presents that are appropriate for eight-year-old boys. We could think about him, what he'd be like at this age, what he might like, and then we could give anything we buy to Toys for Tots in his name."

She stared at him without speaking. This was a nightmare. She was dreaming or something, because she couldn't see Grady being so cruel as to suggest this. "Wh-what?"

"Don't get upset. Just hear me out." He wrapped his hand around his coffee mug and squeezed so hard that his knuckles turned white. "I miss him so much. We—" His voice caught. He coughed to clear his throat and then swallowed a mouthful of coffee. "We never talk about him. I miss talking about him with you. We were his parents and we never talk about our son. It's killing me, Olivia."

"And you think shopping for Christmas presents will help?" Everything inside went cold. She bit her lip hard enough to draw blood. "Why would we do that? How can that help anything? Why would you ask me to do that?"

"To remember our son, Olivia. To do something together with him in mind. To feel close to him around

Christmas." Grady let go of the mug and grasped her hand.
"He loved Christmas, sweetheart. Do you remember?"

"All kids love Christmas," she fired back. "And of
course I remember."

"I want to share this with you. Will you trust me enough
to give this a chance? One hour," Grady pleaded. "Give it
one hour, and if it's too much, we'll stop."

Emotions clogged her throat, tightened her chest. She
shook her head blindly, barely able to see beyond the tears
filling her eyes. "No," she whispered. "No way."

"Just listen," he begged. "I've done this for the past two
years. I'm not going to lie…it was tough the year after we
lost him. It will be tough for you. But sweetheart, I found
that doing this gives me a lot of joy. I want you to feel that
joy."

"*Lost* him? We didn't *lose* him, Grady. Our son died!
He's not hiding somewhere waiting for us to find him."
Her anger shot out before she could edit her words. "He's
gone and no amount of thinking about him or shopping
with him in mind will change that fact."

Grady winced as if she'd struck him. "I *know* he died.
Do you really think I'm capable of forgetting that?" His
Adam's apple bobbed with a heavy swallow. "Look, I
know this is a lot to ask, but if you try, if you go along
with me on this, it might be—"

"Might be what? Painful? Yes! Sad? Yes!" Overwhelming and scary and way, way more than she could handle?
Oh, God, yes. Another round of despair pressed in, rein-
forcing her surety that being with Grady was impossible.
"I **can**'t choose gifts with Cody in mind and give them to
someone else! I can't think about how he would be at this
age, or what he would want for Christmas…or…or…"

She bit her lip harder, willing the tears to recede. Grady
continued to hold her hand, his eyes never leaving hers. A

million and one heartbreaking minutes passed before he said, "Okay, I get it. You're not ready for this. I'm sorry I brought it up." His shoulders lifted in a heavy shrug. "I thought it might help. I hoped... Hell, it doesn't matter. We can do something else."

"No. We can't do something else. I need to go home." She tried to yank her hand out of his grip, but couldn't. "Let go of me," she said between clenched teeth, trying to hold back the gush of tears she felt coming.

"Please stay," he said again. "We don't have to discuss Cody or what happened last night, but I don't want you to leave when you're this upset. Let's spend the day together. We can go see a movie or visit my folks. They're always asking about you."

She shook her head, not trusting herself enough to talk.

"If you leave, it's like we're taking one step forward and two steps backward. Let's not do that. Let's keep moving forward." Grady's voice was even and calm, but each word held the strength of his love, of his conviction that they should be together.

She held her eyes wide open, refusing to blink. The heavy weight of anger dissipated, changing to fear. Not *of* Grady. Never of him. But of what he wanted. Of what she couldn't give him. "We are as far back as we can get. There is no moving forward, Grady. I...I haven't changed my mind about the divorce. I'm sorry for leading you on—" her voice caught as an unwanted sob emerged "—I didn't mean to lead you on, but I still want a divorce."

Grady sat so still, she wasn't sure if he was breathing. But then, "You didn't act like we were making a mistake last night. You had plenty of opportunity to slam on the brakes." Frustration deepened his voice. "Don't do this."

"I have to." She tugged her hand, and he let go. "I don't regret last night, Grady. It was wonderful in...in so many ways. I regret confusing the situation between us…but that's my fault. My mistake. I'm sorry you thought last night meant—"

"I didn't know *what* it meant! But I sure as hell didn't think it meant nothing."

"I know. My fault," she repeated. She hated hurting him, but didn't see a way around it. "It meant something. Of course it did! Just not what you'd like. I really am sorry. So sorry."

"Is this really it, Olly? No turning back here." He held himself stiff and straight, as if pulling all of his strength together to shield himself from her. "You want a divorce?"

Olivia drew in a breath and fastened her eyes on his. "Yes, Grady. I do."

"You're sure?" he demanded. "Be very sure, Olivia."

She swallowed past the lump in her throat. "I'm sure."

His shoulders slumped and he closed his eyes for a millisecond. With a weary, defeated-sounding sigh, he said, "Fine. I can't keep fighting you on this. I'll find an attorney."

More shocked than relieved to hear his agreement, Olivia said, "You will?"

"I will." He looked away. In a lower tone, he said, "I'm sorry."

"For what?"

"For driving the car our son died in."

"It wasn't your fault," she said thickly. He didn't respond, just pointed his gaze toward the door, his message clear. He wanted her to leave. Who could blame him?

She found her shoes and fumbled, nearly falling when she put them on. Opening the door to his apartment seemed to take far more strength than it should. Or, at least, far more strength than she had. Just before stepping outside, she whispered, "I don't blame you, Grady. I blame me. I'm the one who's sorry."

"I can't hear you, Olivia. What did you say?" Grady said.

"I said…goodbye. Just goodbye." She pushed herself out, letting the door slam behind her. The air outside was colder than she expected. So cold, she wouldn't have been surprised if her tears froze on their path down her cheeks.

"So that's it, huh?" Grady's younger-by-two-years brother, Jace, asked from his seat across from Grady. They were eating an early dinner at a local fifties-style diner. Well, Jace was doing most of the eating. Grady was mostly brooding. "Whatever happened to your not-all-alternatives-have-been-exhausted argument?"

"They haven't. But I can't force Olivia to try." Grady shrugged in a vain attempt to appear unaffected by the last twenty-four hours. "So yeah, that's it."

Jace stuffed a few French fries into his mouth, then washed them down with a swig of soda before replying, "That sucks. But I can't say that I'm surprised."

Grady stared at his brother in mild annoyance. "That's some empathy you've got going there. You should quit your job at the paper and become a talk-show host."

"What are you talking about?" To give him credit, Jace looked truly bewildered. "I said it sucks. It does."

"Nice, Jace. My marriage is over and that's the best you have? Even for you, that's a little cold."

"Not cold. It's realistic," Jace said in a firm voice. "I'm sorry for you, but you gotta know that your marriage ended a while ago. At least now, you're not hanging on in blind hope. Frankly, you're better off."

Grady gave his brother a hard stare. "Explain yourself."

"You're not happy. From what you've told me, Olivia

isn't happy, either. The two of you have been stuck in limbo for years. You need to move past this." Jace tossed him his trademark grin. The one that had always served as a get-out-of-jail-free card when they were growing up. "Onward and upward. You deserve to find some happiness. That's all I meant."

Grady swallowed his annoyance. Jace was unencumbered by love and was about as far away from touchy-feely as a guy could get. He also didn't mince words. Which, if Grady was honest with himself, was the reason he'd called Jace to begin with. Tonight, the last thing he needed was touchy-feely. "You have a point," he conceded. "I do want Olivia to be happy again, and I'm obviously not helping in that regard."

"She's not helping, either. You're miserable." Jace wolfed down the rest of his burger before turning a hungry gaze on Grady's. "You gonna eat that?"

Grady shoved his plate forward. "Nope. Go for it."

"Thanks." Jace swapped their plates, saying, "I think I will."

Except for the rumble of other folks chattering at nearby tables, the next few minutes were filled with silence. Shock that he was giving up on his marriage made every muscle in his body ache. But enough was enough. What other option did he have? There was a damn fine line between being hopeful and becoming desperate. He'd already gotten closer to that line than he cared for, but he refused to cross it.

But he'd be lying if he said he didn't feel idiotic. He knew his wife well, and last night wasn't a meaningless romp. Waking up that morning with Olly's legs entwined with his and her head on his chest had given him a sense of rightness in the world that had been missing for too long. It wasn't complete. Nothing would ever feel complete again...not without Cody. But damn, being with his wife again had felt good.

Divorce. The word chewed through his gut like acid. So yeah, as ineloquent as his brother's statement was, Jace was correct. This sucked.

"Don't beat yourself up too much. Hell, from what I can see, most women are contrary, often self-indulgent and experts at playing games with men," Jace said, as if reading Grady's thoughts, albeit a slightly convoluted version of them. "Most of them are just plain crazy."

"Olivia isn't like that. The accident changed her... changed us. It isn't her fault she can barely stand to look at me now."

Jace's hand stilled in the air. "Don't go down that road. You didn't cause that accident. If she blames you for that—"

"She insists she doesn't," Grady said. "But that wasn't what I meant. I remind her too much of Cody. Every damn time I'm in the same room with her, she looks at me and sees him. Can't blame her for that."

Jace leaned back and crossed his arms over his chest, his food apparently forgotten. "She isn't the only person who lost a son. You did, too. Mom and Dad lost their only grandchild, and Seth and I," Jace said, referring to the youngest brother in the Foster clan, who was currently deployed out of the country, "lost our nephew. There's a world of hurt here. It sort of seems as if Olivia is only thinking of herself and what *she* has lost."

His brother's words, no matter how honest and heartfelt they were, irritated Grady. "You're not calling my wife selfish, are you? Yes, you and Seth and Mom and Dad all loved Cody, but it isn't the same. You can't know what this feels like, and I hope you never do."

"Not selfish," Jace said quickly. "But you have to admit

that Olivia has closed herself off from the family. None of us have talked to her in well over a year. Mom and Dad miss her, too." His voice lowered. "Look, I like Olivia. I always have. And I am sick over what you two have gone through. But hell, Grady—what about you? Has she tried to comfort you? Has she tried to be as present in your life as you have in hers?"

Grady didn't answer for a second. In the beginning, right after the accident, she had. They'd tried to comfort each other, had turned to each other, but shortly after the funeral, she'd retreated to a place that Grady couldn't reach. "I don't think she knows how."

"Maybe. But that doesn't make her lack of trying right. And it doesn't help you move on, now does it?"

There was some truth there, Grady admitted to himself. Even so, moving on without Olivia didn't appeal. Sure, visualizing a life without her was possible. Eventually, he'd find a balance and would create a life that made sense. Knowing this, though, didn't make the prospect any easier to choke down. "It is what it is."

"It'll get easier. I don't know how, and I don't know when, but it will," Jace promised.

The sympathy in Jace's eyes surprised him. "Don't look now, but my brother has a heart," Grady teased. "That was bordering on touchy-feely. Maybe you should give that talk-show-host gig a shot."

"Nah. I'm good. My column is doing well and the paper lets me do almost anything I want." Jace tipped his glass and fished out an ice cube. "Can't ask for much more than that."

"That will kill your teeth," Grady said when Jace stuck the ice in his mouth and chomped down. "Hasn't your dentist taught you anything? Women won't find you nearly as attractive with a mouthful of broken teeth."

"Hockey players seem to do okay." Jace became preoccupied with folding his napkin into tiny squares. "Besides, I'm too busy at work and at the house to date much these days."

Even if his brother hadn't avoided eye contact, Grady still wouldn't have believed him. Jace, with his boyish good looks and ramped-up charisma, was a woman magnet. Hollywood would make bundles if they created a reality show based around Jace's extreme dating lifestyle. "You're too busy to date? Right. Tell me another story."

"I'm serious." Picking up his unused fork, Jace tapped it against the table, making a rat-a-tat-tat sound. "And it's not a big deal, so just drop it."

Grady laughed, believing Jace was joking, and fully expecting him to join in. When his brother remained straight-faced, Grady clamped his jaw shut. He was serious? "Whoa. What's up with that? I've never known you to be too busy for women."

Jace lifted his shoulders in a stiff shrug.

Curious about his brother's odd behavior, Grady took a leap. "Have you finally met a woman who refuses to be the flavor of the week?"

"She won't even date me," Jace muttered, clicking the fork harder against the speckled laminate tabletop. "Shoots me down every time I ask. It's exasperating."

"Shoots you down, eh? I never thought the day would come. Who is she?"

Bright splotches of red colored Jace's cheeks. "Someone I work with. No one special."

"Well, you're wrong there." Grady took in his brother's pinched expression. "You're also clueless. A woman who halts your speed-dating lifestyle cannot be described as 'no one special.' Why won't she date you?"

"She thinks I'm a playboy." The admission was made

in a flat tenor, as if Jace couldn't care less. But his tense body language made it clear how very much he did care.

"You *are* a playboy," Grady pointed out. "Anyone who spends more than fifteen minutes with you can see that. So what are you going to do about it?"

"I'm working on that." Jace frowned and a light of anxiety, or maybe it was embarrassment, whisked over him. "Just forget it, okay? Let's talk about something else."

Grady wanted to press harder, but decided not to. Some things a man had to figure out on his own. "Sure. You said something about the house." Jace had bought a fixer-upper a couple of years ago with the intent of flipping the house to make a profit. The slowdown of the economy combined with the fact that Jace loved the location had changed his mind. "Are you finally renovating the place?"

Jace tossed him a grateful smile. "I am. The problem is I tear stuff out and then move on to another room without finishing what I started. Maybe you can swing by and help one of these weekends?"

"Sure." Grady swallowed a chuckle. "Though, if you tear down the entire house and need a place to stay, I have a fairly comfortable couch."

"It won't come to that, but thanks." Jace rubbed one hand over his face and sighed. "I need to take off. I have a column to finish and a couple hours' work planned on the house. You gonna be okay?"

Grady nodded. "One word of advice and I'll leave your women problems alone. If you think you could really love this woman, then she's worth fighting for. If you're not a playboy, prove that to her. If you're serious about her, then show her that."

"Yeah, well…I'm trying." Jace pulled some bills from his wallet and tossed them on the table. "Dinner's on me, seeing as I ate most of it."

Grady watched his brother amble from the restaurant. Seeing Jace like this took Grady back to the moment when he'd finally come to terms with how important Olivia was to him. On some level, he'd known that he'd fallen for her fast, but he hadn't truly realized it until an early autumn morning about six months into their relationship.

She'd stayed the night at his place, and he'd woken up first. He'd stared at her, wondering what demons—real or imagined—made her sleep with her entire body crunched defensively into a ball and her arms shielded over her head. A protective instinct roared to life inside of him. An intrinsic yet indefinable something had altered within him at that very second. And, for better or for worse, he hadn't been the same since.

Not quite ready to leave and go home to his apartment, he motioned for the waitress with his empty cup. In a very real way, he envied Jace. Sure, this woman—whoever she was—might not prove to be anything more than a passing interest, but at this moment, Jace had possibilities that Grady did not.

He wanted those possibilities back, so he went through the previous night and that morning again, remembering every word…every action…every feeling that being with Olivia had stirred up. If only he could find a way to work past the hard shell she'd erected around herself. If only he could find a way to reach her.

The waitress refilled his coffee. He slipped it slowly, his thoughts centered on the problem, his brain searching for an answer. Another two refills later and he had an idea that, if successful, might push through Olivia's walls.

But if he did this, there'd be a lot of anger at first. He could handle her temper, but he'd also have to cause her pain. And that would be devastating. Could he do that?

Begin a path that, no matter how positive the end result might be, hurt the woman he loved?

He thought about the dilemma for a while longer, going over all of the reasons why he should, as well as the very valid reasons why he shouldn't. But as much as he didn't want to hurt Olivia, he kept coming back to one question: If, on the other side of the pain, they could help each other heal, if he could help *her* heal, would the journey be worth it?

The answer was there, staring him down like a friggin' drill sergeant. *Yes.*

And this, surprisingly, had little to do with salvaging their marriage. Yes, he wanted that to happen. Desperately, even. But more than that, he wanted to see his wife smile again. He yearned for her to find a place of peace, so she could also find some level of enjoyment in her life again.

Yes, that was what mattered.

When he finally left the diner, the hope that had disintegrated flared back into being. The hope was slender, but he grabbed on to it with everything he had. Hell, he'd never been afraid of taking chances, but this was a risky game he'd decided to play and the consequences were about as high they could go. And, he admitted to himself as he unlocked his truck, she might even hate him at the end of it.

Chapter Three

Olivia gripped the phone tighter. "What do you mean you won't represent me? You're the best divorce attorney in Portland and you're my best friend. It stands to reason that you would be my attorney for this."

"Calm down, Olivia. I didn't say I *wouldn't* represent you. I said that I had some reservations and I'd have to think about it for a few days," Samantha said in a sooth-ing tone. "If I decide I can't, I'll be happy to pass on some recommendations."

"But I don't want anyone else. I don't think I can do this with anyone else."

"Then you're not ready to divorce your husband," Sa-mantha said in an irritatingly cheerful way. "Which is something you should really think long and hard about."

"I have thought about it, Sam. I'm confused, I guess. I always assumed that you'd represent me, and you never said you wouldn't." Olivia paced the kitchen in an attempt to work out some of her anxiety. "What do you need to think about?"

"Grady is also my friend. It's a personal conflict of interest. I didn't say anything before, because frankly, I was hoping you two would work things out and it would never come to this." Samantha exhaled a sigh. "Besides, whether I represent you or not, I'm still your friend."

Olivia collapsed on one of her chairs. Between yesterday at Grady's and now this, everything was spiraling downhill. "Call Grady yourself. Talk to him about this. You'll see that he's okay with you representing me." At least, Olivia thought he'd say that. After all, he mentioned that he hadn't talked to Samantha in ages, so why would he care? "And now that he's agreed, things will be so much easier."

"Maybe, maybe not. Even with his agreement, you two will have to sit down together to hash out the details. I've done this long enough to know that a friendly divorce is a myth. Things almost always turn ugly when it comes down to deciding who gets what. I really don't want to be in the middle of that."

"He can have anything he wants," Olivia said. "This will be the simplest divorce you've ever handled. I promise!"

"You can't promise that. What if he wants the house?"

Oh. He wouldn't take the house from her, would he? As impossible and heartbreaking as it was to think about her son, this was where Cody was born, where they were happy together. Here, she could almost pretend that the past three years were nothing but a horrible nightmare. Here, she could still feel her son's presence. She couldn't imagine living anywhere else. "Um…"

"See? What if he wants Jasper?"

"Okay, that's just silly. Why would he want the cat?"

"Didn't Grady and Cody bring Jasper home?" Samantha asked. "Wasn't getting the cat in the first place Grady's idea? Now that he knows he won't ever be moving back in, he might decide he'd like to have Jasper for himself."

"That won't happen."

"How do you know?" Samantha pushed. "You've entered into virgin territory, my dear. I'm the expert here, and I'm telling you that people do crazy things in the midst of separating their lives."

"Oh, come on, Samantha! You know Grady better than that. He wouldn't do that to me."

"You've broken his heart, Olivia. You don't know how he's going to react."

Olivia chewed on her bottom lip. Divorce was supposed to ease the pressure on her shoulders and the ache in her heart, give her space to figure out the rest of her life, not increase her struggles. "You really think he'd take my house and my cat?"

"I don't know. But you have to realize that the Grady you know might not be the same Grady you go into court with. I want to support you, but I don't want to turn my back on Grady, either." Samantha sighed again. "I care about both of you. This is a really tough spot for me."

"I get that." It was Olivia's turn to sigh. "How about this? You take some time to think this through, and I'll talk with Grady. I'll see where his thoughts are, and if he's considering yanking me out of my home and stealing my cat away." The words were said sarcastically, as if Olivia thought the entire matter was a joke. But inside, she wasn't laughing. She *had* hurt Grady. And Samantha was the expert on this particular subject. "I-if everything seems okay after I talk with him, will you agree to represent me then?"

"I'd want to talk with him, too. But if that goes well, then yes, of course I'll represent you, sweetie."

Relief filtered over Olivia. If forced, she could get through this using someone other than Samantha as her attorney. Well, she was pretty sure she could. But she didn't want to. All of this was tougher than she'd expected, and having someone she trusted lead her through the maze would make everything a lot easier. "Thank you. I'll call him and see what we can figure out."

"One word of advice. Be ready with a list of your combined property and go through every item together. Don't think anything is too trivial. I've seen tempers flare over something as simple as who gets to keep the twenty-five-dollar coffeemaker."

"I'll make a list and I'll be prepared for a Grady I've never met before. But I don't think any of this is necessary," Olivia said. "We don't hate each other."

"No, my dear. You love each other. And those divorces are always the messiest."

"I think we'll be fine."

Samantha's only response was a very unladylike grunt. Olivia let that go, and instead, changed the topic to something less emotionally draining. After a few more minutes, they finished their conversation and hung up.

Olivia stared at the phone in her hand, considering calling Grady now to set up a meeting for later in the week. But she wasn't ready to hear his voice, so with a sigh, she tossed the phone on the counter and made her way into the living room. Ever since Grady's agreement yesterday morning, all she wanted was to get the process started. To her, it was like ripping off a Band-Aid. The faster you did it, the less it would hurt. That was her hope, anyway.

She'd barely settled on the couch with a book when the rumble of a vehicle turning into her driveway had her jumping up to look out the window. Shivers rolled through her when she saw Grady exiting his truck and heading up the front walk. What did he want? He almost never stopped by without some type of a prior warning.

She gave serious thought to ignoring the doorbell when it rang. Her car was parked in the garage so she could easily pretend she wasn't home. And even though Grady still had a key to the house, he respected her privacy. The bell pealed again. Samantha's concerns reverberated in Olivia's mind. Oh, what the hell. Maybe she and Grady could work some of this out now and get it over with. Before she made it to the door, however, she heard the unmistakable sound of a key turning in the lock.

What in heaven's name did he think he was doing?

Grady waltzed in, caught sight of her hovering near the end of the hallway and gave her the widest grin she'd ever seen. That should have been her first clue. "Hi, honey," he drawled. "I'm home."

"Wh-what?" He certainly didn't appear to be a man with a broken heart.

"I said I'm home." He raised his brows in question. "I rang the doorbell twice. Why didn't you answer?"

"I was busy. And I didn't know you were coming over." She put her hands on her hips in an attempt to ignore the sinking sensation currently developing in the lower regions of her stomach. "And since when do you let yourself in? You don't live here anymore, Grady."

"Oh, but I do. I'm moving back in until we get this divorce stuff worked out. As of now." His stride ate up the floor between them in mere seconds. Leaning in close, he tugged a strand of her hair. "Won't it be fun being roomies again?"

"Wh-what?" she stuttered again. "You're joking, right? You can't do that!"

"Oh, I can. I checked it out with my attorney." Now he chucked her chin, as if she were a child. "This is perfectly legit."

"It's Sunday." She backed out of his reach and instructed herself to stay calm, to focus on the facts. "How did you hire an attorney on a Sunday?"

"She...I mean *he's* a friend of Jace's. Nice fellow and a really smart guy. He gave me some great advice." Grady winked. "Advice I've decided to take."

"He gave you crap advice if he told you that you can move back into a house you haven't lived in for almost a full year!" No way was this happening. Uh-uh. Not if she had anything to say about it.

"But I can. Did you miss that, Olly? I own this house as much as you do, and we're still legally married, we were never legally separated, and none of our property has been divided. So yes, I'm moving in until a judge tells me I have to move out." Grady's grin widened. She sort of wanted to slap him. Hard. "I have some stuff in the truck, but I'll be bringing more over throughout the week."

"No. I won't allow this," she said in a shaky whisper. He couldn't live here with her. No, no, no. Talk about a compromising position. She barely had enough strength to deal with him when she had to, but his being here every single day? No. "Absolutely not."

"Want to help bring a few things in?" he asked as if he hadn't heard her.

"No, I do not! Don't move a muscle, Grady. I'm calling Samantha. She'll tell you that you can't do this!" She didn't give him time to answer, just raced to the kitchen to grab the phone. When Sam answered, Olivia breathed a huge sigh of relief. "Sam?"

"Hey. That was quick. What's up?"

"Grady's here. He says that some crackpot lawyer told

him he can move back into the house." The front door slammed shut. Olivia ran into the living room and peered through the drapes. "Sam! He's bringing in his luggage. You have to tell him that he can't do this."

"Do the two of you still own the house together?" Samantha asked, her voice strangely calm.

"Yes, but—"

"Then he can. He's your husband and the house is his property, too, sweetie. It seems as if he's staking a claim."

"So what am I supposed to do?"

"At the moment? Nothing. But once you hire an attorney, you can ask the court to force Grady to move out for the duration of the divorce proceedings," Samantha mused. "He hasn't lived there for a while, so that might help you. But the facts will come out. He took the apartment to give you space in the hopes that you two could eventually work on your marriage. It's a possibility that a judge won't view that as property abandonment. And trust me, you're better off if you and Grady can decide who's getting what. Don't let a judge make those decisions if you can help it."

Olivia ran to the hallway and pointed to the door when it opened again. "Don't do this, Grady. Please."

He grinned and deposited two large suitcases on the floor. "Any plans for dinner yet? I thought we could order a pizza," he said, before heading back out to his pickup. Forget sort of. She wanted to see her hand mark in glaring red on his cheek.

"You're not eating here!" Olivia hollered after him.

"Olivia? What's going on?" Sam asked.

"He wants to order pizza. To eat. Here. After he unpacks, I'm assuming." She kicked one of Grady's suitcases. Hard. So hard she probably bruised her toe. "He can't stay here."

"He can, Olivia. You can stay with me until you can get a court date, but there's always the possibility that a judge will order *you* to move out. Do you want to take that chance?"

"No, of course not. I'd rather work this out with Grady. And I'm *not* leaving."

"Then you're stuck with him living there for now."

"Great. Just freaking great." Olivia pushed the end button on the phone. When Grady returned with a third and fourth bag, she picked the first two up and dragged them outside.

"Thanks, babe. But that's a little counterproductive. I'm trying to move in, not out," Grady said. "Bring them back in, and I'll get settled. Then we can order a couple of pizzas. Pepperoni and sausage sound good?"

"I say no. Do you hear me Grady Foster? I say no!"

He cocked his head to the side and appraised her as if she were the one who'd lost her mind. As if. "First the chicken marsala and now pepperoni and sausage pizza? You really have changed."

"I'm not talking about the pizza. You. Can't. Stay. Here."

"If you're uncomfortable, I'm okay with letting you live at the apartment while we deal with this divorce business." Grady scratched his chin in thought. "A judge might see that as you not having any interest in the house, though. Is that the case, Olly? Are you giving me the house?"

Oh, God. Samantha had been right. Grady had turned into a freaking lunatic. "Of course I want the house," Olivia said. "And I am not living in your apartment."

Her soon-to-be ex-husband let out an exaggerated sigh. "Then I guess we're right back where we started from. If you don't want pepperoni and sausage, then what?"

"I want you to leave. Please, Grady. Go home."

He gave her a look of false surprise. "You really don't want me to stay here? I could come in handy...your sidewalks need shoveling, for one thing."

"No, actually I do. Every time I tell you to leave, I'm being coy," she snapped. "No, no, no and no I do not want you to stay here."

He entered the kitchen and opened the fridge, grabbing a couple of beers before sitting down at the kitchen table. Jasper, who must have heard the commotion, came in to investigate. Seeing Grady, he leapt into his lap with a meow.

"Well, then let's talk." Grady scratched the area between the cat's ears. Jasper purred like an engine going into overdrive and snuggled in. The traitor. "Maybe we can work something out."

She narrowed her eyes. Her husband was absolutely up to something, but damned if she could figure out what. She hated—oh, how she hated—when he had the upper hand. She almost grabbed her keys and left him there alone, but what would that prove? Only that he'd driven her out of her house. With her cat in *his* lap, no less. Uh-uh.

Giving in, she took the seat across from him. "What do you want? Is it Jasper? Do you want my cat, Grady?"

"Hmm. I hadn't thought about Jasper, but yeah, maybe I do." He slid a beer over to her. "Have a drink. Let's see what we can come up with that will be beneficial to both of us."

She twisted the cap off the bottle but didn't take a drink. "You obviously want something. Just tell me what it is."

"I think the first question to answer is what *you* want. So, what do you want more than anything else right at this minute?"

Cody. Always Cody. Followed by Grady... Well, the

normal Grady. Not this insane version of Grady. "You to get the hell out of this house. Now, preferably."

"See? Now we're getting somewhere. That's a reasonable want, and certainly doable." He swallowed a gulp of beer. "Now, we need to figure out something that will get me to leave. So, Olly. What are you willing to do to put me back in my apartment tonight?"

"I'm willing to not murder you. How's that sound?"

"An awful lot like a threat. I wonder what a judge would say to that? Shall we call Samantha again and get her opinion?"

"No, we shall not." She stared at Grady, trying to read his body language, wishing she could read his thoughts. The only thing she could determine was that he was in this—whatever *this* was—full throttle. And that meant there was no swaying him. Holding her hands up in defeat, she said, "Fine. Why don't you tell me what will put you back into your apartment tonight?"

"I'm not ready to divorce you," he said, as if that were news to her. "But…"

"I'm ready to divorce you."

"Yup. So you can see the problem here. We're at odds. What do you say we reach a compromise?" Grady angled his chair to the side so he could stretch his legs out. Apparently, the movement annoyed Jasper, who jumped down and haughtily stalked off. "I give a little, you give a little. Something for me and something for you."

"Okay, smart man. I know what a compromise is." She wasn't going to like this. But if it would get him out of her house now, then how bad could it be? "Go on."

"For all of this time, I've done what you've wanted me to do. If you said to leave you alone, I left you alone. You said you needed distance, so I gave you that." Grady's gaze soaked into her. "Now, it's time for me to call the shots. For a little while."

"Go on," she repeated. "Just spit it out and tell me what you want."

"To start, we put all talk of divorce on hold for another six weeks."

Ha. She wasn't falling for this. "Nope. You already agreed to the divorce."

"Well, then let me start unpacking, darling. Why don't you order the pizza? Oh, and we're about out of beer. Feel like making a run to the store?" He started to stand, but kept his eyes level with hers. Damn him and his attorney and the horse they rode in on.

"Fine! Six weeks! What else?" She downed a large swallow of beer and waited for the rest of the ax to fall.

"I get six dates with you. My call on when, where and the duration of each date. You can't back out, Olly. If I say we're spending the day bowling in our bathing suits, then you're going to nod, agree and wear a damn bathing suit." He had the nerve to wink. "I'm partial to that purple bikini of yours."

"And if you plan a sex date, do you think I'll just climb in bed with you because you say so?" He wouldn't. She knew that, but he didn't need to know that she knew that.

"Any sex between the two of us will be consenting. Like the other night." He continued to stare at her in that irritating, steady way of his. "What I'm asking for is simple. You give me six dates and six weeks. Then, at the end of those dates and that time frame, if you still want a divorce, I'll sign on the dotted line without one word of dissent. You can have the house and the cat and anything else you want. See how this works? We both win."

Six dates and six weeks, huh? Not such a huge thing to ask, but she didn't want to give it to him. Being cornered pissed her off. Big time. She tried to think it through, tried to reason out what he might be planning to prove to her by doing this, but she came up blank. If three years hadn't changed anything, a month and a half wouldn't, either. "Six weeks is fine, but I only want three dates."

"Nope. But I'm willing to haggle. How about five?"

Five might as well be six, and if she agreed, he was still getting his way. The child in her needed to win on something if she was going to go through with this. "Four dates, Grady. And that's my final answer."

"Four is two less than I was aiming for, sweetheart."

"Take it or leave it. I'm not backing down on this." She mentally crossed her fingers that he wouldn't see through her false bravado. If he pushed, she'd give him the six.

He seemed to consider it, and for a minute, she thought he was going to say no and go about unpacking his things. In her house. But then a satisfied gleam flashed into his eyes and over his features. That's when she knew she'd been had. Damn it! He'd wanted four dates all along.

"All right," he said. "You've got yourself a deal." He stood from the table and threw his empty beer bottle away. "Four it is. Now, how about that pizza?"

"Sure. I could eat." She gave him a slow, sensual smile, hoping to shake the pleased-as-punch look off of his face. "Then we'll be down to three dates. Sounds good to me. Grab me the phone, and I'll order."

A loud burst of laughter erupted from his chest. "Nice try, but pizza tonight is not our first date. You're not getting off that easy."

"Then we're done for now, aren't we? Go home, Grady."

He hesitated for a second, but then nodded and turned to leave. On his way out, he said, "I'd keep your schedule clear. You never know when bathing-suit bowling will strike my fancy."

She didn't bother responding. Once she was alone, she drank down the rest of her beer while waiting for the multitudes of tremors racking her body to cease. In all likelihood, she'd just made another mistake. It probably would have been far smarter, not to mention safer, to have given up the house and stayed with Samantha for a while. Grady probably would've returned to his normal, sane self after a couple of weeks.

But he'd pushed all of her buttons and her innate stubbornness had kicked in. Beyond that, in a weird and maddening way, she found herself looking forward to the next six weeks. Neither the time nor the dates would change anything. She wouldn't—couldn't—let that happen. But the Grady who had strolled into her house was not the Grady she'd known for the past ten years. And yes, he'd frustrated her. Annoyed her. Angered her, even. But he'd also ignited her curiosity.

Who was this Grady? Could there possibly be more to learn about a man she thought she already knew every facet and angle of? Maybe. A tiny amount of excitement thrummed deep within at that thought. And what in the hell did that say about her?

That she was as crazy as her husband. That was what.

Chapter Four

Two days later, Olivia's momentary excitement had vanished under the thick smog of nervousness. She couldn't concentrate, which left her woefully behind in both her transcription duties and the billings for the medical office she worked for. Her employers—a quartet of doctors—hadn't yet noticed her decline in output, but they would if she didn't get her act together soon. Not only that, but she couldn't sleep, eat or focus on anything except for the four freaking dates she'd agreed to.

They held more weight than they should. She blamed Grady for that. Maybe she blamed herself a little, too. She shouldn't have given in so easily. The rat hadn't contacted her since Sunday, so she had no idea what his plans were for their first date. And that annoyed her, because without that information she couldn't mentally prepare herself. Samantha's advice, after she'd finished chuckling at

Olivia's predicament, was to simply phone Grady and ask. Sound advice, perhaps, but also entirely impractical.

Showing her husband the extent of her nerves would only make her more vulnerable, so no—calling Grady was out of the question. Something had to be done, though. After dwelling on the problem all day, she'd decided there was only one avenue left to take. Suppressing a sigh, she turned her compact car into Grady's parents' driveway, parked and turned off the ignition.

Was this a mistake? Maybe. Grady was extraordinarily close to his parents, but she'd kept her distance ever since Cody's death. Not that hard, really. She lived and worked in Beaverton, a suburb of Portland, while John and Karen Foster lived in Northeast Portland. Jeez, when had she last talked to John or Karen, anyway? She thought hard, trying to remember. Dear God, it had been almost two years. How had that much time gone by?

Ugh. She knew how. She'd avoided her mother-in-law's phone calls until Karen had finally given up, and John tended to follow his wife's lead in family affairs. In the beginning, Olivia's actions had been more about survival than anything else. Barricading herself away from others had made sense, especially when dealing with her own emotions took every bit of energy.

Staying away from her family had been easy. She didn't have any siblings and her relationship with her parents was distant, at best. They traveled extensively, and most of their contact came in the form of postcards from various locations around the world.

Grady's family was different. They were the Waltons in living and breathing full color. Grady had pushed for a while, trying to involve her in his family's events, but he'd eventually started visiting his parents alone. Later, after he moved out, avoiding the Foster clan became all that much easier.

So, yeah, even though eradicating Grady's family from her life had basically happened by accident, she doubted she'd be greeted with warmth. Truthfully, she wondered if she'd even be invited in.

Well, she was here now, and while she hoped to gain information that would settle her nerves, she also owed her in-laws an apology. She ignored her trembling fingers and unsnapped her seat belt. Her stomach somersaulted when she walked up the path that led to the Foster's pale-green-shingled Victorian, and by the time she reached the wide front porch, the back of her neck crackled with apprehension.

"You can do this," she whispered to herself. "It won't be nearly as horrible as you think."

Hopefully, anyway. She inhaled a quick breath and raised her fist to knock, but paused when her gaze landed on the cutout, cartoonlike turkey hanging in the window.

In a split second, Cody's voice whisked through her mind. *Why is he wearing a pilgrim hat, Mommy? Turkeys can't wear hats.*

"Because he's only a pretend turkey, and pretend turkeys can wear anything they like," she'd answered on that long-ago morning. Thanksgiving morning, she recalled now. The last holiday she'd spent with her child. Her stomach dipped again and bile coated her throat. This was going to be a hell of a lot harder than she'd thought. She hadn't considered all the memories that being in this house would bring to the surface.

Pressing her lips together tightly, as if that alone would keep her heartache at bay, she held herself firm and rapped on the door. Her mother-in-law swung it open less than a minute later with a wide smile. A smile that quickly disappeared under the mask of stunned surprise.

Karen Foster was still a trim, petite woman whose face showed the signs of a well-lived life. Laugh lines crinkled around her mouth and eyes. Her shoulder-length, dark blond hair was tied away from her face, and other than a few extra strands of silver at her temples, she looked remarkably unchanged. That, along with the turkey hanging in the window, gave Olivia a strange sense of déjà vu.

Karen's brown eyes bore into Olivia. She wiped her hands on the dish towel she held, before tipping her head in greeting. "Olivia," she said in a coolly modulated voice. A voice, by the way, that Olivia had never before heard coming from her mother-in-law. "I wasn't expecting you."

Well, duh. Olivia fought the urge to fidget, and said, "I know. I should have called to…to warn you, but I was worried you might not want to see me."

Karen tucked the dish towel into the waistband of her pink-and-green-flowered apron. She twisted her fingers together, and a silent battle shone brightly in the depths of her eyes. Finally, after what seemed an eternity, she said, "You are always welcome in this home, Olivia Foster. Nothing that has happened will change that you remain a part of this family. But—" she exhaled a noisy sigh "—that doesn't mean I'm entirely happy with you, either."

"I know." The need to run back to her car came on strong, but she held her ground. "I—I understand. I was hoping we could talk."

"I was in the middle of rolling out pie dough." Karen stepped backward and gestured for Olivia to come in. "We can talk in the kitchen."

With a nod, Olivia forced her shaky legs to move and entered the wood-floored foyer. At least her mother-in-law hadn't slammed the door in her face. She kept her vision on Karen's straight-as-an-arrow back as she followed her through the living and dining room, purposely avoiding looking at the family portraits dotting the shelves and walls. The kitchen sat in the rear of the house, overlooking the tree-filled back and side yards with long, narrow windows.

Karen headed directly for the butcher-block island in the middle of the L-shaped room and picked up her flour-dusted rolling pin. Her gaze settling on her hands, she said, "There's coffee made, and plenty of juice and sodas in the fridge if you're thirsty. And if you've a mind to help, those apples could use chopping."

"On it," Olivia said, slipping into her helpful daughter-in-law mode. She grabbed the bowl of peeled and cored apples, dumped the lemon-juice wash in the sink, and then positioned herself in front of the cutting board on the other side of Karen. Within a few minutes, the repetitive motion of slicing combined with the satisfying sound of the knife thunking against the wood-grained board relaxed the tension tightening her muscles.

Silence enveloped the room, each woman involved in their task. That was okay. Olivia used the time to think. There were two conversations that needed to happen here, and she hadn't found the words to begin either of them. Karen must have felt the same, as she seemed content to quietly roll and form dough, filling two pie tins before turning to wash her hands at the sink.

"Those apples about ready?" she asked over her shoulder.

"Other than whatever magic you mix them with to make the filling, yes." Olivia finished cutting the last apple and used the knife to swoop the chunks into the bowl. "How...how have you been? How's John?"

"The same as always, I expect." Karen stood steady, her back to Olivia. "How are you?"

"Fine…I'm fine. Where…uh…where is John? He's retired now, right?" Olivia asked, knowing full well that her father-in-law had retired months earlier, but desperately trying to change the topic. "Is he here?" If at all possible, she'd prefer to say her apologies all at once.

"Jace phoned Sunday night asking for help with his renovation. John's been there all day." Karen's spine stiffened slightly. "He'll be a few more hours, I'd guess." She turned off the water, dried her hands, and then pivoted to face Olivia. "How are you, Olivia?" she asked again.

"Fine," Olivia repeated in a firm voice. "You…ah… must miss him. John, I mean."

"We love each other, but we're not meant to spend every minute of every day together. No couple is. But he'll be home tonight. Time apart is good, but we're stronger when we come together again." She leveraged her gaze with Olivia's. "You could say the same for family."

Okay, then. Her tough-as-nails mother-in-law was not going to be derailed. Olivia pulled the frayed strands of her courage together and said, "I know I've avoided you and John. Jace, too. And Seth, the few times he's been home. But I hope you can understand that I did what I had to do…the only thing I *could* do."

"Avoided us? Is that what you're calling it?" Temper flashed, but Karen quickly masked it. "You didn't only avoid us, Olivia. You ignored us. You cut us out of your life as if we didn't exist. As if we didn't matter."

Olivia swallowed past the thickness choking her windpipe. "One day I was Cody's mother. The next day, I wasn't. I— Knowing who I am if I'm not his mother hasn't been easy to figure out. And being around people who were a part of that other life…it was just too hard."

Karen's head reeled back as if she'd been struck, and unshed tears sparkled in her eyes. "It was hard for us, too. The day Cody was born was one of the happiest of my life. Of John's. We loved that boy, Olivia. His death shredded our hearts." A tear came loose and dripped down her cheek. "It nearly crippled Grady. And your…avoidance nearly destroyed him once and for all."

Okay, she was angry. Olivia hadn't expected anything less. "I did what I had to do," she repeated. What she *still* had to do. "But I never meant to cause more pain."

"You did wrong," Karen said. "I understand that you were hurting, but we all were. Leaning on my family, letting them lean on me, is the only way I've gotten through. But you turned us all away, Olivia. Even your husband."

And that, Olivia knew, was what really bothered Karen. "I'm not like you." Olivia's chest tightened with grief, with the need to explain something that her mother-in-law would never understand. "He was my *son*. I'm not disputing your love for Cody, or your pain, but Karen…he was my son. My child. I've needed time—time alone—to heal. My needs are different than yours, than Grady's. But no one seems to get that."

"Grady's child, too. My grandson. All of us lost him, Olivia. You weren't alone in that. You chose to be alone." Karen's mouth straightened into a thin line. She started to speak again, but instead, grabbed the canister of sugar and a measuring cup.

Olivia clamped her mouth shut against the want to fill the uncomfortable silence. What else could she say, anyway? Karen dumped measured sugar into an empty bowl, her motions quick and efficient. Cinnamon, nutmeg, salt, flour, lemon juice and apple jelly swiftly followed. The tension in the air increased, pressing in around Olivia, making it difficult to breathe, to think.

When the quiet became too overpowering, she said, "I am sorry for hurting you. That was never my intention. I've mostly focused on getting through the days."

Karen gave a short, tight nod before saying, "I may not agree with the path you've chosen, but I accept your apology." With a wooden spoon, she swirled the ingredients together to make a paste, and then dumped the apples into the mix.

"Okay. Good. Thank you for hearing me out. I know it doesn't change the past, but—"

"Though, if you had tried, you might have found that we could have helped each other. You say that being with people who were a part of your life with Cody made things worse, but child, don't you realize that our love for Cody—for you—might have given you strength? Comfort? Family is there through the good and the bad." Karen pointed the wooden spoon at Olivia. "That's what being a part of a family—*this* family—is all about. The same can be said about a marriage."

Ouch. "I haven't broken my vows, Karen. I've done the best I can." Even as she said the words, Olivia's heart and soul knew they were a lie. When she'd promised for better or for worse, through sickness and through health, she'd meant it. Her love for Grady had been so wondrous, so shiny and new and huge, that she'd never thought anything bad would touch them. And really, who ever entered a marriage believing tragedy would strike?

But it had, and as she'd said a million times already, everything had changed.

"Have you, Olivia?" Karen asked, her voice just this side of sharp. But then, before Olivia could answer, Karen said, "Listen to me. I have all these pent-up emotions, and the words are spilling out of my mouth before I can think them through. But what I really want to say is that I'm happy to see you. The rest we can work out, bit by bit, now that you're ready."

Oh, God. Guilt struck Olivia as fast as any lightning bolt could. Of course Karen would think Olivia's sudden appearance meant a reconciliation. Or, at least, a return to some semblance of what used to be. "I've asked Grady for a divorce, Karen. You should know that."

Color drained from her mother-in-law's face. "I see. Silly for me to think... Is that why you're here? To tell me you're divorcing my son?"

"I wanted to apologize. But yes, I also wanted to... Well, stand here and explain myself. I assumed you knew, that Grady had already told you."

Again, Karen focused on her pies, filling one tin and then the other with the apple mixture. Apparently, Olivia wasn't the only one who needed busywork to help clear her mind. After a few minutes, Karen said, "He hasn't said a word. But then, he barely talks about you unless we ask." She looked up, pain and sadness and pity in her expression. "Divorce is so final. Are you sure?"

Well, that was the ten-million-dollar question, wasn't it? "Yes."

"And what does my son have to say about this?"

Olivia paced the kitchen, finding it impossible to stand still any longer. "He argued with me. But he eventually gave in and agreed. I thought the matter was settled."

A glimmer of humor-tinged relief, so slight that Olivia almost missed it, appeared in Karen's eyes. "I take it he's had a change of heart?"

"Yes. He talked me into an agreement that has made me very uncomfortable." Olivia stopped pacing and faced her mother-in-law. "He threatened to move back into the house if I didn't agree!"

"I see." Karen's lips twitched in an almost-grin. "And what would this agreement entail?"

"Four dates and six weeks before moving ahead with the divorce." Olivia approached her mother-in-law, but stopped just shy of arm reach. Mentally crossing her fingers, she asked, "Has he mentioned any of this to you?"

"No, but Grady wouldn't. As I said, he's very private in what he shares about you."

Somehow, this surprised Olivia. She'd thought Grady would've spilled the beans on everything. And there went the hope of getting any info out of Karen. "Look, this whole thing makes me nervous. I don't want to do this. He...tricked me. But I don't plan on these dates changing anything." And then, in a firmer voice, she said, "They *won't* change anything."

This time, Karen didn't bother to hide her smile. This time, the twinkle in her eyes was bright and true and had nothing to do with grief. "Well, then I expect you have nothing to worry about."

Yeah. Right.

Grady parked his truck in the street in front of his parents' house and whistled an upbeat tune. As the owner of Foster's Auto Concepts, he spent his days reconstructing and refinishing high-end luxury cars, both new and vintage. He did a fair amount of work on classic muscle cars, as well. And when the opportunity arose, he bought and sold both varieties. Mostly, though, he loved getting his hands dirty to restore beautiful cars to their former glory.

It was good work. It paid the bills, but more than that, his job fulfilled him on a bone-deep level. What else could a man want from his work? Exiting the truck, he walked around to the front and patted the hood, much like one might pat a beloved pet. His clients thought it odd that he chose to drive a standard pickup, rather than any one of the beauties he'd worked so hard to restore, but he preferred the simplicity of his truck for everyday life.

Separate compartments, he thought, as he meandered up the driveway. Work offered an escape from the structure and emptiness of his day-to-day. Besides, to his way of thinking, it would be a disservice to a vintage Jaguar, a souped-up Charger or a top-of-the-line Corvette to haul him to the shop and back home every day. Or even stored and taken out a few months each year when the weather was good. He supposed he was just too practical, but he damn well appreciated his less-practical customers.

The combination of convincing his wife to delay the divorce and spending the past few days working on a sweet '59 Eldorado had left him in a fine mood. There were few things in life quite as satisfying as a solid eight hours of labor followed up by a well-cooked meal surrounded by family. These Tuesday dinners used to be the norm, but lately, he'd skipped more of them than he'd attended.

Mostly because of Olivia. For once, he had something concrete to share when his folks asked about her. And while he figured they'd be pleased to hear they'd be seeing her soon, he also wanted to give them advance notice. There were far too many unresolved emotions involved to chance an unannounced visit. Especially on Thanksgiving Day, which was his plan for their second date.

But yes, today felt like a good day. A day where anything could happen, and hell, how long had it been since he'd felt that way? His whistling stopped midnote when his eyes landed on the black Civic coupe parked neatly in the driveway. Olivia's?

He blinked. Yep, it was definitely his wife's car. He barely had time to process the strangeness of that when the front door opened. The air carried his mother's voice, and then Olivia's, but not their actual words.

Well, hell. The two most important women in his life had spent how many hours together? What was said? Making a split-second decision, he stepped to the side and took cover next to the car. Olivia choosing today to visit his folks didn't bode well. Was she digging for ammunition to get herself out of their deal? It didn't sound like something she'd do, but he'd pushed her hard. Maybe too hard.

Smothering a curse, he dropped to a crouch and shuffled to the front of the car, intending to get within earshot of their conversation. He doubted his all-about-family mom would side with his wife, but stranger things had happened. And it never hurt to be sure.

"It's too bad John isn't home yet," Mom said to Olivia. "He'd be so pleased to see you."

Thank God she wasn't tearing Olivia to shreds. Grady had worried about that, even knowing how much she loved his wife. Karen Foster had the protective streak of a mama bear when it came to her sons, and she had been quite clear in her disapproval of Olivia's coping measures. The last thing he needed was for Mom's good intentions to send his wife running back to her hidey-hole.

"Why don't you stay for dinner?" his mom asked, her voice breaking into his thoughts. "I've made plenty."

He leaned in closer, hoping to hear Olivia's response. Unfortunately, she spoke low enough that he couldn't. Tightening his body against the side of the car, he shuffled forward a few more inches.

"Idiot," he whispered to himself.

A smart man would walk right up to his mother and his wife and announce his presence. A smart man wouldn't skulk around, hiding behind his wife's car. A compact car, no less.

But he didn't know what had gone on between them in that house. If he still had to play dirty with Olivia, having his mother in hearing distance was a recipe for disaster. He had a healthy respect for his mother, and she wouldn't approve of his coping methods any better than she did Olivia's.

So he waited them out. Soft words were spoken, some he heard and others he didn't. His calves were starting to ache when the front door closed with a thud. He stood quickly and cleared his throat as Olivia came down the front steps. Waved his hand in greeting.

She startled in surprise. For half of a glorious second, a flash of emotion crossed her features, flushing her cheeks pink and deepening the blue in her eyes to a dark sapphire. God, she was glorious. He wanted to walk forward and pull her into his arms. A heartbeat later, she'd assumed the cool facade she normally wore around him. He hated that…the way she'd close herself off and pretend he was a stranger.

"Grady." Stopping about five feet from him, she tightened her jacket belt and then slipped her hands into her pockets. "What are you doing here?"

He shrugged. "It's Tuesday."

"Yes," she fired back, the pink instantly returning to her cheeks. "And yesterday was Monday and tomorrow is Wednesday. Now that we've cleared that up, what are you doing *here,* as in hiding out next to my car?" Narrowing her eyes, she asked, "Were you eavesdropping?"

"Not hiding." He kicked her front right tire. "Your treads are worn." They weren't, but she was unlikely to know the difference. "Bring the car in tomorrow, and I'll replace the tires."

Tipping her head to the side, she gave her car a slow once-over. "You'll have to come up with a better cover,

Grady. The tires are fine. I just had them put on two weeks ago." She leaned her hip against the side of the car and batted her eyelashes. A little move that drove him ten ways of crazy every time she did it. "So, what are you really up to?"

Flat-out ignoring her question, he knelt down and pretended to inspect the tire. She crouched next to him, so close that the scent of her shampoo hit him in the gut. Coconut? Since when? For as long as he'd known her, she'd always used lilac-scented shampoo. The change bothered him, though he couldn't say why. "Who did it?" he asked.

"The tire place on Canyon Road. Why?" Doubt rang crystal-clear in her voice. "Are you seriously telling me they ripped me off?"

Giving up the pretense, he stood and shook his head. "No. You're right. The tires are fine."

"I see. So were you hiding or eavesdropping?" Raising herself to a stand, she fished her car keys out of her purse. "Or both? And why?"

"I was surprised to see you here. You haven't exactly made yourself accessible to the rest of my family. Can't blame me for wondering what *you* were up to."

She stared at him, her chin set and her mouth firm. He yearned to touch her cheek, to rub his thumb along the bottom edge of her lips, to do something—anything—to soften her expression. To make her look at him the way she used to.

"I wanted to see Karen." Her voice hitched, just a little, and that tiny, breathy break nearly did him in. "There's nothing wrong with that."

"Right." The Grady she was accustomed to would accept that answer. Hell, he was proud she'd come here, knowing how difficult that decision must have been. But the old Grady had gotten nowhere with the new Olivia.

So he dug deep, looking for the inner strength to play the game he'd started. "You expect me to believe that after all of this time, you suddenly want to see my parents? Come on, Olivia, spin me another story. What were you doing? Quizzing my mom in the hopes of finding some nugget of information to use against me, so I'll forget about the deal we made? Sorry, but that isn't going to happen."

Anger and shock filtered over her. She stepped backward, as if recoiled by his tone. By his words. He hated himself for that, but hell—it was better than ice. "Who are you?"

"I'm your husband."

"Yes," she agreed, "But you're not the same man I married. Why are you pushing me so hard?"

"Because sitting back and letting you call the shots has only made our situation worse."

"And you think *this* will magically fix everything?"

"You're talking now, aren't you? You're here, and not hiding out at home." Forcing a chuckle he didn't feel, he said, "So yeah, Olly, I think this is a huge improvement."

Every part of her stilled as she appraised him. She tipped her head back, inhaled a breath and blinked once. Twice. He waited for her cool, indifferent mask to slip into place. The proof that she was right—that nothing he did would change anything. The proof that this stupid game he'd started was doomed for failure. Just like everything else he'd tried.

But her face remained flushed, her eyes bright. A visible tremble whisked through her body. Frustration that she couldn't hide her emotions, he guessed. He'd gotten to her. On some level, anyway. And that, right or wrong, pleased him to no end.

"Stay," he said, his resolve newly strengthened.

"For dinner?" Her lips curved into a smile. A luscious,

begging-to-be-kissed type of smile. His gaze fixated on her lips, and just that quick, he lost the ability to rationalize. To think. Hell, to do anything but stare.

He swallowed. "Yes."

In what seemed to be slow motion, she approached him. She fluttered her fingers into his hair, her touch sending him swirling into their past. Long, lazy mornings in bed. Dancing in the moonlight on their honeymoon. A million moments of love and laughter, of promise and passion, ripped through him. And God help him, he couldn't resist those memories. One tug and his lips were on hers. She was so soft. Sweet. Sexy. *His.* Just as much as he was hers.

If only she could see that.

He pulled her tight to his chest and deepened the kiss, savoring her scent, her taste, the pure rightness of holding her. She ran her hands down his back until they settled on his hips. A moanlike sigh escaped from her throat, and his groin tightened in reflex. In want and in need.

In love.

"Stay," he whispered. "Or leave. With me. Whatever you want."

Moving her hands to his chest, she pushed to separate them. She looked up into his eyes. "Sure," she said calmly, if a bit breathlessly. "Dinner with the family sounds like an ideal first date."

He dropped his hold on her and retreated, giving each of them space—though he likely needed it more than she. "Nice try," he said, going for light and easy. "I particularly enjoyed the kiss, but darlin' as much as I appreciate your effort, our first date is already set. Saturday. I'll pick you up at two."

She blinked again. The pink in her cheeks turned a blazing red, but she held her ground. Good for her. "Awesome. Sounds great." Rounding the car, she opened the driver's side door. "Should I wear my bikini, Grady? Would you prefer the purple or the orange?"

He bit back a grin at her sarcastic tone. "Either works for me. I recommend warmer attire, though. We'll be spending the majority of the day outside."

She tossed her hair over her shoulder with the perfected flip only women are capable of. "Can't wait," she said as she climbed into the car. The engine roared to life, and with a little wave, she was gone.

He stared after her for a minute, maybe two, wondering if what had just occurred could be counted as a positive sign or a negative one. The coldness that had surrounded his wife for the past few years seemed to have evaporated. Definitely a positive, there. And that kiss—hell, no way could he describe that kiss as anything less than amazing.

Rubbing his hands together against the chilly air, he headed for the house. He couldn't wait to see what changes Saturday would bring to Olivia. To them. And if a little voice in his head cautioned him about the coming days, he chose to ignore it. Mostly, anyway.

Very purposely, he whistled as he took the front porch stairs two at a time. Her coming here was good, no matter what her intentions were. It was a change from her previous behavior.

He reached for the doorknob, but stopped. A clamp squeezed his heart so hard, he couldn't breathe. The familiar weight crashed onto his shoulders. He grazed the glass window with his fingers, his attention captured by the bright orange-and-brown cardboard turkey.

Why is he wearing a pilgrim hat, Mommy? Turkeys can't wear hats.

"Because he's only a pretend turkey, and pretend turkeys can wear anything they like," Grady whispered, echoing his wife's response from that so-long-ago morning.

Cody had taken that answer as gospel. He'd laughed and darted into the house, looking for his uncles. Jace and Seth had promised to show him a few karate moves, and Cody was not about to let them forget.

Olivia and Grady had kissed. Right here, where Grady now stood. "Let's have a baby," she'd said, her eyes alight with happiness. "A brother or a sister for Cody."

Emotion welled in Grady's throat, hot and fierce. That Thanksgiving had been one of those rare, perfect days you couldn't plan for, couldn't predict.

But damn if he wouldn't do anything in his power to try.

Chapter Five

Olivia stole a glance at her husband and sighed. Grady had arrived at precisely two o'clock, and the nerves swirling in her stomach increased tenfold the second she'd opened the door. Being this nervous was ridiculous, but he looked so *good*. Dressed in standard blue jeans, a thick flannel shirt and the leather jacket she'd bought him years earlier, he shouldn't have looked any better than any man, anywhere.

But he did. He was Grady. And now, fifteen minutes of driving later, she'd be willing to swear thousands of butterflies were zipping around inside of her. Why oh, why couldn't she have married a less handsome man? While she was at it, she wished he was less tenacious, less intelligent and less charming. Oh, and if he could please have a normal, everyday-sounding voice—one that didn't unhinge everything inside of her—that would be helpful.

Of course, these attributes were only a small part of

the reason she'd fallen for him to begin with. Add in his honorable nature, his sense of humor and his unwavering commitment to anything and everyone he cared about, and she was a goner before she'd even realized it.

Simply speaking, she had never met a better man. A man who deserved far more than she was able to give.

"Why so quiet, Olly?" Grady asked as he stopped at a streetlight, his tenor seeping into her like bubbly water. Not just any water, either. But some type of expensive, sparkling water that originated in a faraway place only inhabited by mystical, magical creatures. "I figured you'd be laying down the rules for the day by now."

"I thought you were calling the shots. Isn't that what you said?"

"It is, and I am. But since when did that stop you?"

"Never." Another sigh begged to be released, but she squelched it and faced the window to stare at moving pavement. The only rule she had was to keep any discussion of their son off the table, but she figured Grady wouldn't agree to that. So why bother? "Nope. No rules."

"I'm surprised." He reached over to squeeze her hand. "But I'm glad to hear it."

She tugged out of his grasp and turned on the radio. Christmas music blared from the speakers, loud and cheery. She flipped it off immediately. "It isn't even Thanksgiving yet," she said, as a way to explain her behavior. "Way too soon for 'Jingle Bells.'"

"That wasn't 'Jingle Bells,'" Grady said. "I believe that was—"

"Doesn't matter." The song was "Frosty the Snowman." Cody's favorite. "Still too soon."

Thankfully, he didn't argue with her or try to engage her in further conversation. She *hated* this time of year. Christmas songs, Christmas movies, Christmas lights,

Christmas food and Christmas decorations. Christmas, Christmas, Christmas. She wanted to go to sleep and wake up in mid-January, when the world returned to normal.

They drove for another ten minutes before Grady slowed the truck and pulled off to the side. He switched off the ignition and tucked his keys into his front pocket. "It's a beautiful day, isn't it?"

Olivia took in her surroundings before narrowing her eyes at Grady. Yep, Samantha was right. He had most definitely lost his mind. "It's cold, gray and windy."

"That it is," he said with an infuriatingly cheerful smile. "But I'm with you, and that makes any day beautiful."

Telltale heat infused her cheeks. Great. She was likely as red as a fire engine. "Um. Well. That's nice of you to say."

"It's the truth." He opened his door. "I have a few things in the back I could use your help with."

A heavy dose of confusion replaced her anxiety. "Our date is *here?*" He nodded in response. She strove for calmness. "Grady, it's *really* cold and windy."

"Don't worry. I'll keep you warm."

"I didn't mean… I don't need you to—" He exited the vehicle before she could finish. Okay, then. She followed suit and met him at the rear of the truck. "It's the middle of November," she pointed out. Any reasonable person would understand what she was getting at.

"Yep. You're right on that, too." Apparently, Grady had lost his sense of reason along with his marbles. He grabbed a large, zippered bag from the bed of the pickup and held it in front of her. "This is lighter than it looks. Mind carrying it?"

"Pretty sure I can manage." She accepted the bag and hefted it over her shoulder, all the while trying to stare him down. He, naturally, appeared oblivious. "What exactly are we doing here, Grady? Have you planned a picnic or something?"

"Or something." He lifted a medium-size cooler with one hand, and then another large bag with the other. "Ready?"

"For?" Again, he took off without answering. Damn him. She chased after him, the cold wind strong enough that she had to push against it. When she finally caught up, she said, "What are we doing at a park in mid-November on a cold, blustery, cloud-filled day? You know, they said it might snow later."

"Nah. It's not quite cold enough for snow. Might get some rain, though." He stopped and glanced at her. "I told you to dress warm."

"And I listened, but I didn't bring an umbrella."

"Quit complaining. You forget how well I know you. A little cold rain never stopped you before. Remember that camping trip in Washington we took the year before we were married?" He winked and tossed her the smile that melted her bones. "You didn't seem to mind the rain or the wind then."

How could she possibly forget that trip? They'd huddled together in a tent to stay warm. Well, they did a lot of other things to stay warm, too. She shook her head and tried to focus. Better not to think about those days. "That was different. I have no idea what we're doing here."

"I told you. We're having our first date. That's all you need to know until you know more." Another wink and he started walking again. At a slower pace, thank goodness. "I promise you'll enjoy yourself, Olivia. If you'll relax and let me take control…even if only for the next several hours."

His tone wasn't flippant or condescending. She didn't hear anything but hope and quiet resolve. In a way she didn't comprehend, that alone softened *her* resolve. That morning, in an effort to quiet her whipped-up nerves, she'd promised herself—again—that nothing Grady could do or say would alter her decision. And she believed that. Her plan had been to push against every obstacle he put in front of her, but maybe that was the wrong way to go. Maybe she could use these dates to show *him* they couldn't create a new future with the pain of their past.

Turning the tables so she came out ahead. She liked that idea, if for no other reason than it gave her an objective, rather than fretting over his. And her chance at success would be a heck of a lot better if she softened her defenses. Go along for the ride, so to speak. Giving it her best shot, she said, "You win. I'll do this your way."

This surprised him enough that he paused for a heartbeat to glance in her direction. "I'll hold you to that."

They continued walking for a few more minutes before she realized where they were headed. Oh, dear God. This wasn't only the first date of the four she'd agreed to, her demented husband was re-creating their *very* first date. A bubble of apprehension tightened in her chest. This wasn't ideal.

"A baseball game?" she asked as they got closer to the ballpark. "Are you serious? In November?"

"I believe we've already established that the month is, indeed, November. And yes, a baseball game."

"How in the hell did you find a team that was playing this time of year?"

"I have my ways." He tipped his head toward the bleachers. "Come on, let's find a seat."

"Right, because there are so many people here." Like four others, maybe. "We better hurry." He didn't dignify her sarcasm with a reply, so she followed. Why did his choice of a baseball game bother her so much? Probably because it was wholly unexpected. She'd anticipated Grady to woo her with romance, but this—a trip down memory lane that didn't involve their son? "You're crazy," she murmured. "And we'll freeze."

"I might be a little crazy," he agreed. "But you don't have to worry about freezing."

He led her to a seat and deposited the cooler and the bag he carried before reaching for hers. "I brought blankets, hot chocolate, and—" he unzipped one of the bags and pulled out two nylon bags "—these." With finesse, he removed a rolled-up seat cushion that had a battery of some sort attached. He fiddled with it for a second before placing the thin cushion on the bleacher seat. "For you, milady," he said with a gallant bow.

She squinted at the seat and then back at him. "Heated seat cushions?"

"It is November, Olly." His lips twitched in mirth. "Kind of cold for a baseball game."

"Exactly what I've been saying," she mumbled. "So… uh…how long will these stay warm?"

"Long enough."

She sat down, determined to do whatever it took to get through the day. "Did you say you brought cocoa?" she asked in as cheery a manner as possible.

"I did. Two thermoses full, even."

In less than five minutes, she was as snug as a bug in a rug. She shouldn't have been surprised at how well Grady had thought everything through. But somehow, she was. He'd left nothing to do with their comfort to chance. She had a thick, thermal blanket wrapped around her shoulders, a cup of hot chocolate in her hands and her bum wasn't cold in the least.

Taking a small sip of her beverage, she looked out toward the ball field. The players were teenage boys, and the only way to tell the teams apart was by their baseball caps. One team had green bills and the other black. "How did you set this up?"

"No questions, Olly. Remember, you're doing this my way."

"Right." She huffed out a breath and tried, oh, how she tried, to relax.

"You don't have to talk to me. You don't even have to look at me if you don't want." He swore under his breath. "If it will make you feel better, you can pretend you're here all by your lonesome. I'm just some stranger who chose to sit next to you."

She laughed. She couldn't help it. "Seriously?" Because she had a difficult time believing that Grady had gone to such extents without expecting *something* from her. "I don't have to do anything but sit here?"

"Why does that surprise you?" Annoyance colored his words and his jaw firmed in frustration. "I am not the bad guy. I thought—" He coughed, as if to clear his throat. "I thought it would be a nice change of pace to do something fun."

"I never said... I don't think you're the bad guy, Grady." She shifted her eyes downward, away from his focused attention. "It's just..."

"Just what?"

Oh, to hell with it. "You make me uncomfortable, okay? I can't relax around you. I don't know how to do that. Not anymore."

"How do I make you uncomfortable?"

"I don't know!" Ugh. That wasn't the complete truth. "Whenever we're together, I'm reminded of how much I've let you down because I can't give you what you want." She gestured toward the ball field. "Like this. I don't know what you think is going to happen with these dates, but whatever it is—it isn't going to. I am not capable of being who you want me to be. So I'm going to let you down. Again. And yes, Grady, that puts me on the defensive whenever we're in the same room."

He stroked the bottom of her chin with his fingers. Gently, firmly, he applied the smallest amount of pressure so she had to look up. "Take a breath, sweetheart," he said, looking directly into her eyes. "It is impossible for you to let me down. I promise you that all I want is to kick back, enjoy the game and hopefully leave us both with some nice memories. Trust me on this, Olly. Have a little faith. Please?"

He meant it. She could see the conviction of his answer in the steadiness of his gaze. She could hear it in the even tenor of his voice. "All right. I can do that."

"Good. Then we're all set." Releasing his grasp, he faced front. "They're about to get started."

So Olivia watched the ball game and tried to forget about the blowing wind, the gray skies and the confusing, sexy man sitting next to her. She kept waiting for him to bring up Cody, but he didn't. He also didn't touch her or try to create a sense of intimacy. He simply watched the freaking ball game as if he were sitting in front of his television at home.

Which was good. That was what he'd promised, after all. But his actions didn't ring true to her, even if his proclamation had. Every now and then, she'd slide him a sidelong glance, but he never noticed. Or, if he did, he pretended he didn't. After a while, she gave up and allowed herself to completely focus on the game.

The players were good, she noted, functioning together as a team should. In fact, she'd bet money that the two teams were actually one, but had split into two units for the purposes of this game. Perhaps Grady hadn't set this up, as she'd originally thought. Perhaps this was nothing more than an off-season scrimmage meant to keep the team in shape.

Out of nowhere, a memory of her first date with Grady overtook her. They'd gone to a Beavers game at PGE Park. Up until then, Olivia had only seen baseball played on TV, and truthfully, she'd never understood the appeal. When Grady had invited her to a ball game, she assumed she'd feel the same. She was wrong.

There was something very different about viewing a game—any game—live and in person. The excitement in the air, the cheering fans, the varied expressions on the players' faces—from intense when they were down in runs, to jubilant when they pulled to the top—had quickly made her a fan.

Grady had fed her hot dogs slathered with mustard, which they washed down with ice-cold beer. And when the team had hit a grand slam, he leaned over and kissed her. The second their lips touched, she was swept away. Never had she felt such an instantaneous connection to a man. Their relationship had proceeded forward without a glitch from that moment, and truly, their life had been like a fairy tale.

Somehow, sitting here with Grady almost made her feel like the girl she was back then, when everything between them had been brand-new. When her dreams for the future were still possible...when she believed in happily ever after.

"It's close," Grady murmured, putting an end to her reminiscing. "Who do you think will win?"

"The teams seem equally matched." She swallowed a gulp of cocoa. "But my money is on green. The pitcher has a strong arm."

"Yes," Grady agreed. "But the black team's pitcher isn't a slouch, and their batters seem more consistent."

Well, he had a point. But, "I still say green."

"Any reason why? Beyond the pitcher's strong arm?"

"Call it a feeling." Her lips twitched in unexpected humor. "And you know, I'm right with these feelings more often than I'm wrong." Counting off on her fingers, she said, "Baseball, football, hockey...heck, even soccer. How often have my feelings proved to be right? Hmm, Grady? I seem to recall weeks and weeks of you slaving over the oven as a result of your choosing the losing teams against my winning ones."

Not to mention the long, luxurious massages she'd also won. Massages that always led to... Yeah, better to keep those memories to herself.

"You just have an inordinate amount of good luck when it comes to sports. Or perhaps I enjoyed preparing dinner enough to have let you win," Grady teased. "But this time, I'm sure of it. Black will come out on top."

"Wanna bet on that?" A true, to-the-tips-of-her-toes smile emerged. God, she'd missed this easy camaraderie. Who would've guessed? "Say twenty bucks?"

"Twenty? That's child's play. If we're going to bet, let's do it in style."

"Oh, yeah? And what do you have in mind?"

"If I win, I get a kiss."

She spurted not-so-hot chocolate from her mouth. Awesome. That had to have been attractive. Wiping her mouth, she said, "A kiss? Umm..."

"If you're not confident in your choice, then I suppose we can settle on twenty dollars." He scraped his thumb along her bottom lip. Desire—unbidden and heady—uncurled from the center of her belly. "Missed some."

"F-fine," she stammered. "If you win, you get a kiss.

I win and I get—" she thought hard, trying to find some-thing weighty enough to make the bet worthwhile "—one less date! Instead of three more, you get two."

Throaty laughter tumbled from his gorgeous mouth, but he nodded. "Heavy stakes, Olly, but I'll take your bet. If green wins, we're down to two dates. After this one, of course."

"Of course."

The game continued on, and a large portion of Olivia's reservations melted away. Heck, she'd kissed him the other day, so what was she out if she lost? Nothing, really. Well, okay, that was a lie. Kissing him at her in-laws had been a spur-of-the-moment action, one that she regretted. Kiss-ing him again was so not a good idea.

But if she won… Well, that was one less date she'd have to struggle through. Decent odds. But it made her wonder why he agreed. She knew he wanted them to rec-oncile, but maybe his secondary goal was nothing more than to spend some time with her before they went their separate ways? Maybe he needed these dates for closure? The thought gave her pause. She'd been so wrapped up in what she needed, she hadn't given much consideration to what Grady might need. "Selfish," she whispered.

"Hmm, Olivia?" Grady asked.

"Nothing. Just…you know, talking to myself." Yes, she'd definitely behaved selfishly. The realization of that made her feel about two inches tall. Still, she also didn't see how she could've done anything different under the circumstances. But if it was closure he was after, she could certainly give him that.

As long as he didn't talk about Cody, or take her shop-ping for Cody, or anything else related to their son, that is. Thinking of Cody dropped her mood by several degrees, so she shoved everything except for the game out of her head and returned her attention to the ball field. The two teams had stayed in pace with each other for a while, but her team had just moved ahead by one run. When they were up by two, she stood and cheered.

"Told ya," she said to Grady, retaking her seat. He offered a wink in response.

A strong blast of wind hit her face and lifted her hair. Shivering, she pulled the blanket tighter around her. Grady gently pried her mug out of her frozen fingers and refilled it with hot chocolate, but her concentration was so great on the game, she almost didn't notice. They were finally in the last inning and the green team was up by three runs, but the black team had the bases loaded. If the next batter hit a home run, and therefore, a grand slam, the black team would win. And she would have to share a kiss with Grady.

But come on, how often did grand slams happen? It couldn't be that often. Especially with a high-school baseball team.

The makeshift umpire, probably one of the coaches, called "Batter up!" and she mentally crossed her fingers, toes and all other appendages. Without thought, she grabbed Grady's hand and squeezed. He squeezed back. She angled forward, every part of her intent on the pitcher, and prayed the batter would miss. He swung high but the ball came in low.

"Strike one!"

"He missed that one by a mile," she said to Grady. The batter tapped his bat against the ground and then raised it to his shoulder. "Green's going to win and we'll be down to two dates."

"Shh. Just watch," he replied. "I have complete faith in my team. Black will win and you'll owe me a kiss, darlin'."

The batter swung low and fast, but the pitch was high. "Strike two!"

"I'm going to win," she said in a singsong voice. "And you are going to lose."

"Maybe," Grady replied in a not-worried-at-all tone. "Maybe not."

"He isn't reading the pitcher well, Grady. He's the last batter, and this is the last swing." The batter took his stance again, and his teammates hollered out their support. "The writing is on the wall, and it says—" Her jaw fell open when the batter expertly smacked the ball, the resounding crack seemingly deafening, and the ball flew across the sky. Even in her distress, she had to acknowledge it was a perfect hit. "No way," Olivia whispered as each base plus the batter ran the diamond to home. "No freaking way."

"You were saying, Olivia?" Grady dropped her hand and leaned in close. So close, they were nearly lip to lip. He certainly wasn't wasting any time in claiming his spoils…er, his kiss. "The writing says what, exactly?"

"Umm…" Again, she was taken back to their very first kiss when they also sat in the bleachers. When his eyes met hers and the lazy, humdrum beat of reality had ceased to exist.

His head came closer, closer. And then, closer still. Her breath locked in her chest. One sensation after another tore through her, and—loath as she was to admit it, even to herself—she yearned for his kiss. For *this* kiss. Craved it, really. Unable to hold herself straight, she fell slightly forward, tilted her head up and closed her eyes.

She trembled in traitorous want when she sensed his mouth hovering over hers, when his cheek scraped against hers in a tantalizing, barely there brush.

"I believe the writing says that I won," he whispered.

His warm breath sizzled against her cold skin, warming her from the inside out, filling her with that unconscionable need that never completely dissipated. "What do you think of that, Olly?"

"I think if you're going to kiss me, you should get it over with." The quicker the better, please. Waiting for it... Well, that might just kill her. A rumble of laughter forced her eyes open. "What is so funny?"

"You make me smile. Is that such a terrible thing?" Wind tumbled her hair forward. He carefully tucked the stray strands back in place. "But no. I am not going to kiss you right now."

She rolled her bottom lip between her teeth and tried to ignore the studied way in which he appraised her. "But you won."

"So I did," he said as he shifted away.

"Then kiss me, Grady." She puckered her lips and leaned forward. He—damn him—laughed again. Upset and strangely disappointed, she angled her arms over her chest and frowned. "If you don't want to kiss me, why did you make that your bet?"

"I didn't say when I would kiss you, did I?" He busied himself with folding their blankets and tucking them into the bag. Reaching over, his hand brushed against her thigh. Every muscle in her body tightened at his touch. "Just trying to—" his fingers found the cushion she sat on and he tugged "—put everything away."

"Uh-huh. Sure you are." But she moved so he could grab the cushion. Within minutes, he was standing with the cooler and one of the bags in his hands. "Come on. We have dinner next."

"Dinner? No! *This* was our date, Grady." She motioned to the now empty ball field. "And now it's over."

"Part of our date. I promised the guys food."

"Promised the guys? What guys?" But then, she knew. He meant the teams. "You *did* set this up, didn't you?"

"Well, it isn't easy to find a game this time of year," he acknowledged.

"We could have gone to a movie," she grumbled. "Or... um...bowling."

His gaze, hot and searching, skimmed over her. "Can't get that bowling-in-our-bathing-suits idea out of your head, can you? But as appealing as the idea of that is, my goal wasn't to make you uncomfortable. Besides which, date number one had to be this." With that, he started down the bleachers, confident that she would follow.

Well, duh. If she wanted to get home, she didn't have a lot of options. Stifling a curse, she picked up the bag he'd left behind and stalked to where he waited. "What do you mean it had to be a baseball game? Why?"

He shrugged and in a light, easy tone, said, "Today needed to be about something fun, something we've shared in the past that didn't hold even one painful memory. Our first date was magical, Olly. For me, anyway."

Every defensive edge softened. "Me, too," she admitted. "And I did have fun, so thank you." Then, remembering her goal to go along for the ride, she continued, "And not only am I famished, but I'd love to meet the team."

"Perfect. They're waiting at a picnic area straight ahead." The corners of his lips turned upward in a lopsided grin. *Cody's* lopsided grin. "Hope you're in the mood for a barbeque."

And just that quickly, her good mood was destroyed. But she smiled anyway. Nodded. Cody would have loved a barbecue at the park in November.

Well, then, so would she.

Hell, if she could enjoy herself at a baseball game the weekend before Thanksgiving, why not a barbecue? Besides which, she planned on quizzing the boys to find out exactly how Grady had coerced them into playing today. She was pretty sure it wasn't because of the promise of grilled hot dogs.

Two and a half hours later, they finally pulled into Olivia's driveway. The day hadn't been nearly as horrible as she'd originally imagined. In fact, she could even say she had fun for a good portion of the hours she'd spent with Grady. The key was to focus on the present. Granted, this was much easier accomplished when Grady wasn't within seeing, smelling or hearing distance, but she'd mostly managed. And she hadn't cried once. Progress.

She'd even learned more about her husband. It turned out that Grady was one of the volunteer coaches for the high school team that played for them. Apparently, he'd started his coaching gig the previous spring, and he seemed to have developed an excellent relationship with his players.

None of that surprised her. Not really, anyway. Her husband was built to be around kids, no matter their age. And one of his favorite father-son activities had been teaching his son about baseball. So the fact that he'd decided to coach made perfect sense. What had surprised her, though, was how willing the boys were to give up a Saturday afternoon at Grady's request.

She didn't know that many teenagers, but it seemed to her that giving up a precious weekend day to help out their coach—with no reward other than a few hot dogs—spoke volumes.

"Those kids are great," she said, unbuckling her seat belt. "Thank you for introducing them to me."

"You're welcome. I think they had a good time. I hope so, anyway."

"Oh, they did! I…um…didn't know you'd started coaching. I think that's great, Grady. Really great. They're lucky to have you."

He shrugged off her compliment. "I'm the lucky one. I do this for me." Before she could ask him what he meant by that, he leaned across her to open her door. "I'll walk you in."

"Not necessary!" Ack. Way too loud. Lowering the volume, she said, "I'm fine. Thank you, though."

"I'll walk you to the door," he said again in that firm, no-nonsense way of his.

"Really, Grady. There's no reason for you to. I am perfectly capable of letting myself in to my house. I do it nearly every day."

"*Our* house," he said softly. "But I won't come in if that's what you're worried about."

Um, no. What she was worried about was that damn kiss. The one he still hadn't claimed. "I wasn't worried." She stepped from the truck and waited for him to join her. It took only a few seconds to reach the front door. "So… when is our second date? I have a lot going on at work and I might have some late nights. I might even have to work weekends. Busy, busy."

"I don't think you'll have any problems with time off for what I have planned." Oh-so-carefully, as if she were made of china, he gripped her shoulders and tugged her toward him.

Oh. He was going to kiss her. Right now. Myriad emotions enveloped her—desire, frustration, want, need and a fair amount of denial. Okay, oodles and oodles of denial. She licked her lips and straightened her shoulders.

She could do this without falling apart. A bet was, after all, a bet. And she'd lost fair and square.

"I'm ready, Grady." She arched her back, closed her eyes and licked her lips again. "You can kiss me now."

"Are you sure?" His warm and teasing voice forced a tremble through her body.

"Very. Let's get this over with. Before I—"

"Before you...what?"

Die from waiting. But she refused to say that. Instead, she went with, "Freeze to death. So come on, let's do this. Otherwise, I'm going inside."

A breath wheezed out of her chest when he ran his thumb over her cheek. When he laced his fingers into her hair and tugged her head toward him. She felt the heat of him as his face neared hers, and her entire body thrummed with energy. Why did her body crave him so?

His lips grazed her forehead in a sweet, quick kiss before moving to the tip of her nose. He kissed her there, too. Her knees weakened to the consistency of butter, and she had to push her back against the porch railing to stay upright. She waited breathlessly for their lips to meet, but instead, he dropped his hold on her and moved away.

"There," he said gruffly. "Consider your debt paid in full."

She blinked open her eyes in stunned disbelief. "That's it? That was the kiss I waited all day for?" Oh, crap. She hadn't actually meant *waited.* More like *worried* about.

"Whenever you want a real kiss, sweetheart, all you have to do is ask."

"Right. Well, that won't be happening." He'd kissed her nose, for goodness' sake. Her nose! "You know, I just figured you'd...um...take full advantage."

"You figured wrong. The next time we kiss, it will mean something, Olly."

"Uh-huh. Okay, then." God, since when had she become such a bumbling fool around him? She blinked in an effort to find her balance, to shield herself in the way she had for the past several years, but found she was too flustered. "I'm…um… Just let me find my key."

"I have mine right here." Reaching over, he slid the key in and pushed the door open. "Thank you for today, Olly. It meant a lot to me."

"It was fun!" A shiver stole over her.

"You're cold. Go inside and take one of those bubble baths you love so much." With that, he turned on his heel and headed for his truck. "Oh, and our next date is Thursday," he called over his shoulder. "Say around noon."

She didn't respond. Couldn't, really, what with so many bewildering thoughts clouding her head. He tooted his horn lightly as he backed out of her driveway. And then he was gone. Numb, confused and, yes, disappointed—though, she couldn't say why—Olivia let herself in and locked the door. Jasper was waiting for her, hungry for attention and food.

"I know, I know. I left you alone for too long. You can blame Grady for that one." She bent at the knees to pick the cat up. Rubbing her chin against the top of his furry head, she whispered, "You're the only guy I need. You never ask more of me than I can give, and you keep my feet warm at night. Why, Jasper, I think you just might be the perfect male."

He meowed, as if in agreement, and then pounced out of her arms and raced to the laundry room, which was where she kept his food. Knowing there'd be no peace until she filled his bowl, she fed him, gave him fresh water and then took the stairs to her bedroom.

It was nearing seven o'clock, but it might as well have been midnight. Her face felt chapped from the hours spent outside, her muscles were tight and knotted from stress and an overabundance of emotions, and her heart ached with a heaviness she couldn't identify.

"Just tired," she mumbled, heading for the bathroom. She'd take a hot bath, as Grady had suggested, and then go to bed early with a book.

It wasn't until she was up to her chin in bubbles that she finally comprehended Grady's parting statement about their next date. "Oh, hell, no!" Thursday was *Thanksgiving*.

He expected her to spend Thanksgiving with him… with his family? That holiday of all holidays? Impossible. "No, no, no," she said, sinking deeper into the tub. She hadn't celebrated Thanksgiving or Christmas since Cody's death. Everyone around her understood her reticence over Christmas, but no one seemed to get that Thanksgiving was almost more painful.

How could it not be when the last Thanksgiving she'd spent with her family had been the happiest of her life? Then, she'd had plenty to be thankful for: a good marriage, a healthy and happy child, the possibility of a second child and a love she was sure would last forever.

But without Cody, she had nothing to be thankful for. All she had left were memories.

Her plan for *this* Thanksgiving had been the same as the last two: spaghetti, red wine and an action movie marathon at Samantha's. She sat up so fast that water splashed over the side of the tub. She had plans already! Grady couldn't possibly expect her to cancel at his whim, could he? That would be unfair to Samantha.

She would call him first thing in the morning. Surely, he'd agree to another day for their second date. But then, she recalled the Grady she was dealing with. Maybe he *would* let her off the hook, but he'd probably insist on another four dates and an additional six weeks—or something else equally as ludicrous.

Oh, hell, indeed. Thanksgiving. With her in-laws. In a house that had held many a happy family gathering. Memories: they were going to be her undoing, one way or another. She was sure of it.

"Damn you, Grady."

Chapter Six

Samantha Hagen was a petite blonde with jade-green eyes, a Cupid's-bow mouth and a sultry, come-hither voice that tended to stop men in their tracks. She was a barracuda in the courtroom, but as a friend they didn't come any better.

She was also single, mostly because of her horrible luck with the opposite sex. Some men couldn't handle her brains. Others couldn't deal with the fact that she earned more money than they did. And then there were the guys who appreciated her intelligence, had great careers, but couldn't seem to get a grip on dating a woman who looked like Samantha.

Of course, that was how Samantha explained her single status. Olivia thought there was a lot more to it, but she didn't pry. That road went two ways.

"Everything is going to be fine, Iris," Samantha said into the phone. She smiled at Olivia and gestured for her to sit. "I understand you're anxious. Let me explain the process again."

Olivia slid into a chair to wait. It was Monday afternoon. Samantha's office was a twenty-minute drive from where Olivia worked, so she had to take an extended lunch break for this meeting. Likely, she'd have to stay late to make up the time, but this was important.

Grady, naturally, had refused to bend on his Thanksgiving Day date, so she had to cancel with Samantha. That wasn't the only reason Olivia needed to talk to Sam, though. She also wanted her to draw up the divorce papers, so when the six weeks were up, Olivia would have them ready to go. That is, if her friend had decided to represent her.

"Iris? I'm sorry, but my next appointment is here. May I call you back in an hour or so?" Samantha jotted herself a note. "Yes. One hour." Hanging up the phone, she took a large gulp of water before saying, "Some days, I feel all I do is talk, talk, talk. Most days, I wonder if half of what I say is even getting through."

"I've often thought you're as much a counselor as you are an attorney," Olivia said. "And people tend to tune out what they don't want to hear."

"Yes! That's it exactly." Samantha twisted the cap onto the water bottle. "The negativity wears me down. I suppose I should be used to it by now."

"I think your clients are very smart for choosing you."

Samantha chuckled. "I recognize kissing up when I hear it. And yes, I've talked to Grady. He's fine with my representing you."

"Okay, good." Olivia suddenly felt ten pounds lighter. "What about you? Are you comfortable acting as my attorney?"

"Well, we need to have a conversation about that," Sam admitted.

Uh-oh. This didn't sound promising. "Look. If you're uncomfortable, I get that. Your friendship means more to me than anything else."

"That isn't what I said, Olivia." Sam stood, rounded her desk and took the seat next to Olivia. "But, hon, I have to be honest. I wonder if you're as sure about this course of action as you say you are. It's a huge step and you and Grady—" She shook her head as if to gather her thoughts. "I've never seen two people as happy together as you two were."

"You're right. We *were* happy. But Sam, I can't keep having this conversation. Everyone asks me if I'm sure. Everyone reminds me of how we used to be." Olivia sighed. "I'm trying to look forward."

"But *are* you sure?"

"Do you ask all of your clients that question?"

"Actually, I do." Samantha reached out, as if she were going to touch Olivia, but pulled back. "I admit that I'm personally invested in your well-being. You're like a sister to me. But if you can't give me a straight answer, then I won't be able to represent you."

"I'm sure, Sam." Olivia spoke firmly, with as much conviction as she could find. The pressure on her heart increased. "I promise you that this is the right decision for me."

Disappointment flashed over Sam's face, but she nodded. "Then I guess you've hired yourself a lawyer."

Another ten pounds disappeared. "Thank you," Olivia said.

"So, we should set up a meeting for late December or early January." Sam returned to her desk. Staring at her computer monitor, she said, "I have a lot going on at the end of December, so let's plan for early January? That will give you time to settle the details with Grady. Then, it's just a matter of going over what you've agreed to, and I'll be able to get the papers ready for your signatures."

"What? No. I want you to do that now. That's one of the reasons I'm here."

"But you promised Grady you'd hold off for six weeks," Sam pointed out. "It's only been one, which leaves another five weeks before you can officially begin the process."

"I told him I'd hold off, yes. I never said I wouldn't prepare." Olivia tried to keep her frustration from showing. "He's already talked to some crackpot attorney, remember?"

"Oh, I doubt she…he—whatever—is a crackpot." A tinge of pink colored Samantha's cheeks. "I'm sure the advice Grady received was…um…well thought out. And with the best intentions. Only the best."

Narrowing her eyes, Olivia said, "Oh, come on! Telling Grady he should move back into the house? That's—" She broke off. "Wait a minute. I don't care who his attorney is. That isn't why I'm here. All I'm asking is for you to get everything ready—whatever that entails—so when the time comes, I can *officially* get the ball moving."

Sam's shoulders firmed. "What, exactly, did you agree to? Because I think you're walking a fine line here, Olivia."

"All I promised is I would 'put off all talk of divorce' for six weeks and four dates. I don't see how having the papers ready to go when that time frame is up is walking a fine line."

"Well, you're wrong. We are talking. And the topic is divorce, right?"

"With you. I'm not talking about it with *him*."

"Definitely a fine line." Samantha slid a pad of paper

in front of her and grabbed a pen. "But I suppose you're standing on the right side of that line, so I can't really argue. Please tell me you've had some type of discussion with Grady regarding your joint property?"

"Yep. He said I could have anything I wanted."

Sam scrawled something on the pad. "And what is it you want?"

"The house and the cat. That's it. But I want to buy out his portion of the equity in the house. That's only fair."

Sam made another note. "What about his business? You used to keep the financials for Foster's Auto Concepts, and you helped him get the business up and running. You're certainly entitled to a portion of the company."

"I'm not interested in that," Olivia was quick to say. "That's his. All his, Sam."

"It really isn't. Your involvement in Foster's Auto Concepts was substantial. You worked side by side with Grady for years, Olivia." Samantha chewed her bottom lip. "With any other client, I would push hard for this. You could receive a tidy lump sum to remove all further claims to the business, or you could keep your claim and receive a percentage of the profits each year."

"No." She shook her head vehemently. "I will not take any part of Grady's company. Not now, not ever." She'd already taken enough from him.

Sam's mouth wiggled in a tiny smile. "Hmm. If that's the case, then I don't think we should offer payment for the house. You keep the house, he keeps the business."

"No," Olivia said again. "When this is over, I want to feel that the house is really mine. And I won't unless I buy out his interest."

"He probably won't accept money from you."

"You'll have to convince him, then. Or his attorney. But this is the way it has to be, Sam. At the end of this, I need to know that I've done right by Grady. As much as I can, anyway." Olivia dug in her purse for the packet of papers she'd brought with her. When she found them, she pushed the envelope they were encased in across the desk to Samantha. "I had the house appraised six months ago, when I thought about selling it. Here are the documents, along with information about our mortgage."

Sam picked up the envelope but didn't open it. "Basically, this will be as simple as it gets, then. I'll figure out an appropriate offer, draw up the papers, and once each of you signs, that will be that. Other than the waiting period." She leveled her gaze with Olivia's. "You might change your mind. What if you regret this decision down the road?"

"I won't." A lie? Maybe. But Olivia already had regrets that ran much deeper than going through with a divorce. She needed this. Grady, even though he couldn't see that yet, needed it, too. She was doing this for both of them. "Really."

With a shrug, Sam ripped off the paper she'd written on, paper-clipped it to the envelope, and slid both into an empty file folder. "I'll have something to show you within a few weeks. Maybe more, but definitely before Christmas."

"That's it? Really?"

"If what you've told me is true, then yes. But don't expect the emotional process to be as easy as the legal process. You might find this much more difficult than you think."

Well, she already knew that. "It won't be any more difficult than anything we've already gone through."

Samantha's eyes softened. "I know." And, because she was such a terrific friend, she didn't expand. "So, I think that's it? Do you have time for a quick lunch?"

"Unfortunately, no. I need to get back to work. But—and I'm so sorry about this—I have to cancel our plans for Thanksgiving. Apparently, Grady has decided that we should spend the holiday together for our second date."

She expected Sam to appear shocked. Or disappointed, at least. Instead, she nodded. "That's right. He told me."

Okay, that was a surprise. "How often have you guys talked lately? When we went to dinner the other night—thanks for that, by the way—he mentioned he hadn't spoken to you for a while."

Another shrug. "A few times, I guess. Grady felt bad and wanted to make sure I wouldn't be alone for Thanksgiving, so he ran his idea by me."

Gee, yet another surprise. "So you've known about this for how long?"

"Last week. Monday, I believe. But he asked me not to tell you until he had a chance to run it by his folks." Samantha's complexion paled. "I shouldn't have said that. See? This is why I was worried about representing you. I love both of you, Olivia. And yes, our friendship is closer than my friendship with Grady, but I feel loyal to him, too."

One breath, then two. "It's okay. I'm not angry, Sam. I was just shocked to realize that you've known about his Thanksgiving idea for longer than I have. That you didn't tell me right away." She smiled to soften her words. "But I understand the tough position you're in, so we're fine."

Relief washed over Sam's face. "Good. Besides, Grady also invited me to Thanksgiving at his parents. I was going to say no, but if you want—"

"I want! Absolutely. Please be there. You'll make the day so much easier if you're there."

"Then I'll accept his invitation," Samantha said without missing a beat. "And I'm not letting you off the hook, either. I look forward to our annual action movie marathon, and I had some great flicks lined up for this year."

"Of course. Name the day and I'll be there."

Suddenly, the prospect of spending Turkey Day with Grady and her in-laws wasn't nearly as terrifying as it was before. Thank God for Samantha.

John Foster opened the door with a delighted smile and a twinkle in his ocean-blue eyes. His boys may have gotten their mother's eyes, but their height, bone structure and everything else came from their dad. Olivia smiled in return. Something about her father-in-law always brought out her good side. He had this wondrous skill for making people feel at ease.

"Happy Thanksgiving, John."

"It does the heart good to see you, Olivia." John pulled her into one of his trademark bear hugs. She had to shift the container of cookies she held so they wouldn't get crushed. Oh, jeez, he smelled the same. Like coffee and peppermint. "I've missed you," he said.

"I've missed you, too," she said as they separated. And she had, even if she hadn't realized how much until exactly that second. "You're looking good." His hair, which he wore cut close to his head, had whitened to the color of a fresh snow. It suited him. Beyond that, he looked happier than she remembered. Less stressed. "Retirement must agree with you?"

"It does," he agreed, motioning for her to enter. "Come in, come in. It's a gorgeous-looking day out there, but a mite too cold for my taste." Cocking his head to the side, he glanced over her shoulder. "Where's that son of mine?"

"Oh. I'm sure he'll be along shortly." Olivia had woken up edgy and distracted, so she'd decided to drive herself to Thanksgiving. She'd called Grady to tell him, but he hadn't answered. So she left him a sticky note stuck to her door, which would probably annoy him. But, hey, it wasn't like she reneged on their deal. She was here, wasn't she?

Besides which, driving herself made her feel more in control. Even if she wasn't. And knowing it would bug him made her feel better, even if that was a little petty.

Smiling cheerfully, she held out the container. "I brought some cookies for later. Should I put them in the kitchen?"

"That will be fine. I was sure Grady said you two were coming over together," John said, the gleam in his eyes growing brighter. "I expect he'll be surprised to find that isn't the case?"

Her father-in-law had always been extraordinarily intuitive. "Well, you know. I was ready to leave and he hadn't shown up yet. So here I am." Balancing the cookies in one hand, and then the other, she removed her coat. "But I left him a note."

"Good. Glad to see you're keeping him on his toes," John said with a laugh. He took her coat and hung it in the closet. "Come on, let's sit down and get reacquainted."

Wow. He truly seemed happy to see her. It was almost as if the past three years hadn't happened. Dangerous thoughts to have. Thoughts she *shouldn't* have. "Um… sure. Just let me take these to the kitchen."

"I have a better idea. Let's take those with us. Karen's shooed me out of the kitchen all morning, and I'm starving. I'll get you some coffee, and we can sit in front of the fireplace. You take it light, no sugar, correct?"

She nodded and went to wait in front of the stone fireplace. The mantel was decorated with a host of family photographs. She knew without looking that her wedding photo was one of them, as well as one of her and Grady with Cody shortly after his birth. Kicking off her shoes, she curled her legs beneath her and stared at the fire. She was not going to allow herself to become overwhelmed so early in a day that promised to be a struggle.

John returned with coffee for both of them. She accepted hers and took a fortifying gulp. "Help yourself," she said, nodding to the container she'd placed on the table between them.

"Karen will be out in a bit. She's just put the turkey in the oven."

"I should go help—"

"She'll let you and me and anyone else who is here know when she's ready for help. But she says hi and welcome."

"I'm glad to be here. It's… Well, it's been too long."

John set his coffee down and cleared his throat. "I'm not the type of man who sticks his nose in where it isn't wanted." Leaning forward, he said in a soft voice, "I don't need to when my wife takes care of that for me."

She grinned, because she knew John expected her to. "I have a suspicion that you two work quite well together."

"Aye. I suppose that's true." Her father-in-law sat straight and contemplated her. "Please forgive me for butting in this one time, Olivia. You're just as beautiful as always, but you look tired and, if you don't mind me saying, you're a bit on the pale side," he said in a gruff tone. "I've worried about you. We… Well, we haven't been able to take care of you. I hope you're taking care of yourself in our absence."

"I am. Or I'm trying to." Such a sweet, sweet man. A small glow of warmth unfurled inside. She breathed in a lungful of air. "Grady isn't making it any easier," she confided. "But don't you tell him I said that."

"Well, he's a stubborn man. Takes after his mother in that regard."

"Oh, I think we can safely say some of that comes from you, too," she teased, hoping to ease the press of emotion weighing in the air. "In fact, I'd say all three of your sons have that stubborn streak."

"True enough." He removed the lid from the plastic container and took a cookie. "Pumpkin spice?"

"Yes. I remembered how much you like them." It was odd, baking the cookies she'd always brought to the Foster Thanksgiving, but old habits die hard. The last time she'd made them, Cody had cracked the eggs. This time…well, it was just her.

"I was hoping you would." John bit off a large chunk, chewed, and then said, "Have one, Olivia. You could use some fattening up."

A laugh slipped out, surprising her. "You said that to me the very first Thanksgiving I was ever here." And nearly every time he'd seen her from then on. "I'm glad I came early," she said. "I'm enjoying spending this moment with you."

"So am I, Olivia."

"You've always made me feel at home here," she confided. "Don't get me wrong, Karen and Jace and Seth always have, too. But with you…I don't know, I guess I felt a connection to you right off the bat. It just took a little longer with everyone else." She sighed. "That didn't come out very well, did it?"

"Oh, I think you did a pretty good job of it. And the feeling is mutual."

"I'm sorry, John. For removing myself from everyone's life," she said, knowing now—when they were still alone—was the best time to offer him the apology he deserved. In this instance, she didn't feel the need to offer excuses for her behavior. John wouldn't require them. He tended to accept people for who they were: good, bad or somewhere in between. "I hope you know I never meant to hurt anyone."

"I know, and thank you for the apology." He chewed the remainder of his second cookie and swallowed some coffee before continuing. "It isn't necessary, though."

"Yes, it is. For me."

"I understand. More than you know." Pain and sorrow lurked in his quiet timbre. "You and me, we're fine. I do have a favor to ask of you."

"Sure. If I can."

"Don't forget you have family who loves you. I am quite sincere in this, Olivia. Despite what happens with my son, I will always consider you my daughter." The front door opened, sending a blast of cold air into the room. John winked at her. "Got it?"

Maybe she was wrong. Maybe she did have something to be thankful for today, after all. "Got it."

Grady strode into the living room from the foyer, caught sight of her and stopped. "So you are here."

Yep, he was annoyed. Oh, well, she couldn't really blame him. "I'm supposed to be, aren't I?"

"I was supposed to pick you up, wasn't I?"

"Don't tell me you're seriously upset I drove myself," Olivia said. "I tried calling and I left you a note. Besides which, you never said that riding with you was part of the date."

John pulled himself to a stand. "I'll leave you two alone." On his way out, he frowned at Grady. "Play nice or I'll tell your mother." Then, to Olivia, he said, "And you—remember that you loved him once, even if you don't love him now."

John left the room, but Olivia barely noticed. She was too busy staring at Grady. He went from annoyed to impassive in two seconds flat, and his eyes...they were dark and cold. And he was looking at her as if she were a stranger. In all that had happened, she'd never seen him look at her that way. It was…disquieting.

"I didn't say that," she whispered. "I don't know why your father—"

Grady gave a stiff shrug, as if his father's statement meant nothing to him. Maybe it didn't. Maybe he was finally beginning to see that memories weren't enough to hold them together. "Doesn't matter. If he believes you don't love me, there must be a reason. I guess I'll have to think about that."

She opened her mouth to tell him he was wrong, that she had never stopped loving him, that she likely never would stop, but had second thoughts. Not because she enjoyed hurting Grady, but because professing her love at this point would be the same as leading him on. And wouldn't that only serve to hurt him more in the long run? So she mimicked his shrug. "Believe what you want, but I'm not going to stand here and argue over it. I'm also not going to apologize for driving myself here."

"I wouldn't expect you to." He closed his eyes for a second and pushed out a long, drawn-out sigh. "You don't need to, either."

"Glad we've cleared that up." She stood. "But now I'm going to go help your mom in the kitchen."

He looked as if he were going to argue, but the doorbell rang before he could. Talk about good timing. "That would be Samantha," Grady said. "Why don't you let her in, and since you obviously don't want to be around me at the moment, *I'll* go help in the kitchen."

For a day that had begun better than she'd expected, it sure was spiraling downhill fast. "This is your family, Grady. I don't want to ruin Thanksgiving. How about if Sam and I take off? I'm sure she won't mind."

"*I'll* mind," he said, his voice just this side of brusque.

"But if having me here is going to be too difficult now—"

"Everything is difficult with you, Olly." He combed his fingers through his hair in frustration. "Every. Damn. Thing."

"You're no walk in the park, either, buddy," Olivia said, her flippant tone meant to hide her own bruised feelings. She wasn't sure she pulled it off. The doorbell rang again, followed by two sharp knocks. "Shall I tell Sam we're taking off?"

"No. We made a deal, remember?"

"Like you'll let me forget!"

"I have to! Why did you bother agreeing if you were going to continuously try to get out—"

"That doorbell is giving me a headache!" Karen's voice swept into the room before her physical form. She stopped at the threshold between the dining room and the living room, her complexion a good two shades paler than normal. "Is there a reason you're not answering the door?"

"It's Samantha, Mom. We'll…I'll let her in," Grady said quickly. "I can see her car from here, so I know it's her."

Karen's shoulders sagged. "See that you do. It is bad-mannered to keep her waiting while you two squabble like a couple of children."

"Sorry," Olivia and Grady said in unison.

"This is a day of thanks. I would appreciate it if the two of you could start behaving like the family we are, instead of trying to one-up each other." With her hands on her hips, Karen glowered at both of them. "If you can't say something nice, then keep your mouths closed. Or, if you absolutely must go at each other, do so outside where I can't hear you."

Lovely. Just lovely. Upsetting her mother-in-law had not been on Olivia's agenda. "I'm sorry, Karen," she said again. "You're right. We'll behave."

"Yes, Mom. From here on out. Promise," Grady said.

Karen nodded and returned to the kitchen. When they were alone again, Grady said, "Look. I don't want you to leave, and I don't really care how you got here."

"Fine. I—I suppose staying isn't a horrible idea," she relented. "And it would be discourteous to leave now."

He dipped his head so she couldn't see his face. Was he smiling? "Yup, that would be rude."

"Okay. So that's settled." She tried to walk past him, but he stopped her by stepping in front of her. Every instinct she had begged her to tell him the truth, that she was happy to be here, that she wished with every one of the 206 bones in her body that their lives could be different. Of course, doing so would be foolhardy, so she didn't. "What now? Sam's probably freezing out there."

And, as if Samantha could hear their conversation, the doorbell pealed. Again.

"Will one of you answer the dang door?" Karen hollered. "Before I—"

"We're getting there, Mom!" Grady called out. He set his hands on Olivia's shoulders. "One question—we had fun the other day, right?"

"Yes."

"Then try to do the same today. Date number two, Olly." He swallowed hard enough that his Adam's apple bobbed. "After this, you're halfway to that divorce you want so much."

"Right." Halfway to the end. That should've been the

good news, so why did it feel so horrible? "I'm counting the days." Twisting away, she went to let Samantha in.

"You do that," he said from behind her. "I'm counting on us."

Chapter Seven

Her hair still smelled like coconuts instead of lilacs, and it still bugged the hell out of Grady. Obviously, this was beyond stupid and nonsensical. Asinine, even. Why should he care what scent of shampoo Olivia used to wash her hair? There weren't any clear answers. And hell, even that bothered him. He hated when he couldn't make sense of something. Almost as much as he hated not being able to fix something.

A lot of both going around lately. Especially where Olivia was concerned.

The woman in question was currently playing a game of UNO with his mom, dad and brother. She was smiling, laughing and apparently having a great time. Which was what he wanted, wasn't it? Yes. But he'd hoped to be a part of that equation.

Kind of difficult when she'd avoided even standing in his general vicinity ever since their discussion—

argument?—earlier. They sat next to each other for Thanksgiving dinner, but it was either that or create a fuss, which Olivia was unlikely to do in front of his family. Throughout the meal, she'd barely spoken to him. Everything she said had either started with "Pass the" or "You're welcome."

"You're behaving like an imbecile." Samantha smacked him on the knee to get his attention. They were sitting in the living room, supposedly watching a television program. "You and I both know she hasn't stopped loving you. Your father was probably trying to wake her up. Or you. Or both."

"Maybe." Grady stood to add another log to the fire. When he returned to the couch, he said, "Probably. But that isn't what's bothering me."

"Then what is?"

"She isn't using the same shampoo," he muttered. "And I've always taken care of her car, but she took it somewhere else to have the tires changed."

"I see," Samantha said, completely straight-faced. "Yes, both of those things should cause you great concern."

"They are! And I can't figure out why—" He stopped, looked at Samantha's expression, and sighed. "Ah, I see. You're showing your sarcastic wit, aren't you?"

Samantha snorted. "What do you think? So what if she changed her shampoo? Maybe her stylist suggested it, or maybe she got a great deal, or maybe it was a gift, or maybe she felt like a change. Women do that. As to the car…I'm sure that was more about asserting her independence than anything else." Scooting forward, Samantha picked up her glass of white wine. "So, what else you got?"

"She's been telling me for months that she's changed, that she isn't the same woman I married. I'm starting to believe her." Frustration pooled in every syllable. "You spend more time with her than I do. What do you think?"

"Like I said, you're behaving like an imbecile." Samantha gave him a look filled with pitied humor. "You've changed, too. Hey, guess what? I've changed since you two were married. Everyone in this house has." She smacked his other knee. "It's called life."

"Right, and that's what I thought she meant. But I don't think so, Sammy." He looked toward the dining room again to be sure Olivia was focused on the game. Lowering his voice, he said, "I'm beginning to think that the core of who she is has changed. And I don't mean the obvious. Cody's death changed the way I look at life…hell, the way I look at everything. But I can find joy in my memories of him. She can't. It's as if life has lost all meaning for her. And that scares the hell out of me."

"If that were the case, she wouldn't get up in the morning. She wouldn't be able to hold a job. She wouldn't take care of herself." Samantha shook her head. "She's still the same girl inside that she always was. She's fighting hard to make peace with…with fate, I guess. She's just…lost, and trying to make sense of something that is impossible to make sense of. It's up to the people who love her to show her the way."

"And God knows I've tried. I don't know, Sammy. Today certainly isn't turning out as planned." He shifted away from Samantha. In case she was rearing up to hit him again. "Maybe *I'm* holding her back. Maybe I'm making it more difficult for her to find peace." He cursed under his breath. "Hell, maybe it's time I listened and gave her the damn divorce."

"You might very well have to, but not today. Not tomorrow, either." She clicked her nails against the side of her glass. Looked at him as if trying to make her mind up about something, and then shrugged. "She came to my office on Monday…in an official capacity."

Hearing that had about the same effect as getting beat across the head with a two-by-four. In other words, it woke him the hell up. "Why?"

"Remember, I said 'official capacity,' so I can't tell you. But I will say that if you're unhappy with the current status of your second date, then why are you sitting here moping?" Angling her head toward the dining room table, she continued, "I have never known you to walk away from anything. So…I don't know, Grady, get in there and change things."

"Any ideas on how?" Grady grabbed Sam's hand a millisecond before it made contact with his thigh. "Why do tiny little blonde women think it's acceptable to pummel a man with their tiny little fists?"

"Because we grew up defending ourselves from groping hands," she replied with a grin. "But point taken. As to your question, how much do you love her?"

"So much that—" Breaking off, he closed his eyes for a second to find the right words. "I love her enough to walk away if that is what she needs. I love her enough to give up my happiness in exchange for hers."

"Aw, Grady, you're breaking my heart." Samantha reached one hand toward him. He tensed, sure she was about to smack him again. Instead, she laid her palm on his cheek. "She doesn't think she deserves your love anymore." Then, holding her hand up to stop the question she somehow knew was coming, said, "No. She's never said that to me so bluntly, but it's the truth. And I don't know why she feels that way. If I were going to give you any additional advice, I would suggest trying to figure out why she might have that mind-set."

Grady had nothing to say. He couldn't imagine why

Olivia would feel that way. Sammy had to be wrong. Hadn't he told Olivia over and over that he loved her, that he would do anything in his power to reconcile? It was much more likely that Olivia believed he didn't deserve *her* love. And hell, if she felt that way, what was he going to do?

Olivia laughed from the next room, and his heart pinged. "I need to get to the truth. Whatever that is," he said to Samantha. "Thank you for listening."

"I'll send you my bill next week," she said dryly. "Have I properly motivated you?"

He thought about that. Yes, the day had started off badly. So what? Thanksgiving wasn't over yet. He still had time. "Why are you helping me? She'll kill you if she finds out."

"Jeez, man, keep your voice down!" Sam swallowed a healthy portion of her wine. "Besides, I'm not *really* helping you. I gave you some advice about joint property and how you could possibly use that to your advantage. I didn't suggest that you trick her—you had that idea before you called me. And I'll tell her that if she ever asks."

"Why are you helping me in *any* capacity, then?" It seemed to be his lot in life to deal with one confusing woman after another.

"Because she's my family and she loves you. Because I deal with couples who don't love each other every day of the week. Because maybe you two had something that few couples do. I hate to see that go to waste." Sam shrugged again. "Simple as that."

"I don't think so." He leaned over and tugged her hair. "You're a romantic, Sammy-girl. I don't think I knew that about you."

"Yeah... Well, don't spread it around." She sniffed.

"I have a reputation of being a coldhearted man-hater to maintain."

"Our secret." He laughed as he stood. "Okay, here I go. Wish me luck."

She raised her nearly empty wineglass in a faux toast. "Go get 'em, tiger."

Optimism somewhat returned—thanks to Sammy. He went to join his wife. His plan *was* working. Olivia was bonding with his family, as if no time at all had passed. And that was a big part of what he'd hoped to accomplish with date number two.

Now he had to remind her that this was, indeed, a date. He needed to get them back to where they were on Saturday, because date number three was fast approaching. And that was the big one. That was the one that would cause some damage. If he and Olivia weren't to a certain point by then, he doubted they'd get to date number four.

Hell, if things went way south, he'd be lucky if she was even willing to talk to him again.

Olivia drew four cards and scowled at Jace, who was seated to her right. "How many of those hideous cards do you have?"

"Are the—" Jace paused and squinted at her cards "—multitudes of cards you're holding weighing you down?" he teased. "You know what they say, if you can't take the heat, stay out of the kitchen."

"You just wait. Someone will toss a reverse out there, and then you're all mine," she teased right back. Other than her skirmish with Grady that morning, the day had been a delight. Cody, naturally, was a constant presence in her mind and heart. In order to stay sane—and make it through the day—she'd allowed herself to settle in to the crazy rhythm of the Foster family.

Weirdly enough, it had worked.

Waving her cards in front of Jace, she said, "You think I'm only holding number cards in this hand? Hmm?"

"Oh, I see how it is—" Something behind Jace caught his attention. He nodded, shrugged and laid his cards face-down on the table. "Actually, I'm done for now. Gonna go hang out with the pretty blonde in the living room."

"She'll eat you alive, Jace," Olivia said. "Proceed with caution."

"You can't leave! We're in the middle of a game," Karen interjected. John elbowed her and rolled his eyes toward Jace. A millisecond later, a mile-wide grin appeared. "Oh…are you taking Jace's place, Grady?"

Olivia swiveled in her seat to see Grady waiting in the wings. Oh, no. This wouldn't do.

"I am," Grady said. "You guys are having way too much fun in here for me to miss out."

"Grady, why don't you take over my hand?" she asked. "That way, Jace can keep playing and I can visit with Samantha."

Her brother-in-law scraped his chair backward. "Nah, I'm good. I could use a break."

Grady slid his long-legged frame into the chair Jace vacated. "Thanks, bro. And I'd listen to Olly if I were you. Sammy's a sweetheart, but she's tough. And a fair amount smarter than you. Way out of your league."

"My league doesn't even begin where yours ends," Jace fired back. And then, realizing he'd put down Olivia in the same breath as his brother, he backtracked. "Umm… I'd date you in a second, Olly. Really. I don't know how he won you over in the first place."

Olivia laughed, instantly feeling more at ease about Grady being so close. Somehow, she'd missed the sibling bickering, too. She really was as crazy as her husband.

"I suppose my pride should be bruised, but it isn't. Besides, are you talking minor or major league? Sam and I are definitely in the majors. And...umm...let's just say the few dates of yours I've met...not so much."

John chuckled from his place across the table. "Yep, the girl can still hold her own."

"I'm at a loss," Jace admitted. "Anything I say will either compliment Grady or insult you, so I'm going to say nothing, make a graceful exit and keep your major-league friend company."

"He really isn't going to make a play for Samantha, is he?" she asked Grady after Jace disappeared into the next room. Softly, of course, so John and Karen wouldn't hear. "I like your brother a lot, but Sam doesn't need to fall for a player."

"Actually, Jace claims he isn't a player," Grady said just as softly. "He's set his sights on a lady he works with. He's stopped dating altogether because she won't go out with him."

"Really? Wow. I never thought... Wow."

"My thoughts exactly."

"You two going to play or gossip about your brother's love life?" John asked in good-natured humor. "Leave him be. He'll figure it out on his own."

"Umm, right. Of course." Olivia's entire body flushed warm with embarrassment. "Sorry."

"There's a woman that Jace is interested in?" Karen sighed when John elbowed her again. Then, switching her attention to Grady, she said, "Later, I expect you'll share with me whatever you know about this woman. Every last detail. You say he works with her?"

John winked at Olivia, as if to remind her of their conversation earlier—the one about sticking noses into other people's business. She winked back.

"Yup. That's what he said, anyway." Grady picked up Jace's discarded hand and whistled. "But now you know as much as I do, so there's nothing left to tell you."

"There has to be some—"

"Let's play already, for cryin' out loud." John nodded to the discard pile. "It's your turn, son. And it looks as if your mother has a few of those Draw Four cards, as well."

They finished that game—Karen won—and were in the process of beginning another when the telephone rang. From Olivia's vantage point, she could clearly see the full-on desperation that overtook Karen's features. A shiver of foreboding ran down Olivia's spine.

"Do you think?" Karen asked John, who was already up and moving toward the kitchen. "Is it possible?" Jumping up, she followed her husband out of the room.

"Jace! Get in here," Grady hollered, rising to his feet. "Hurry."

Dread struck Olivia fast and hard. Throughout the entire day, as much as everyone smiled and chatted, there had been an obvious absence. Seth, John and Karen's youngest son, hadn't been able to get home for the holiday. He was in the air force, and was currently deployed in Afghanistan.

A sick feeling churned in Olivia's stomach. Her skin suddenly became cold. Clammy. She couldn't bear to think…to consider what might be happening. Falling in behind Grady and Jace, she raced to the kitchen.

Her mother-in-law's back was braced against John's chest, his arms were wrapped around her and the phone was pressed to her ear. Tears cascaded down her cheeks. Olivia's heart thumped and nausea climbed her throat. Karen was trying to talk, but seemed too overwhelmed to form actual words. With sadness?

Oh, God. Oh, no.

Not again. Olivia couldn't go through this again, couldn't see someone she loved going through this. Her gaze found Grady, but his attention was wholly centered on his mother.

"What's going on?" Olivia whispered. "Is… Seth?"

"Yes, it's Seth," John said. "We hoped to hear from him today. Now, our Thanksgiving is complete."

It took longer than it should for John's statement to make sense in Olivia's muddled brain. Seth was on the phone and not some anonymous person delivering horrifying news about him? A relief so great she almost keeled over rushed through her. God, for a second there, she'd thought… Well, she'd thought a mother's worst nightmare had come true. Again.

Her knees weakened to the point she thought she was going to collapse, so she backed out of the kitchen and retook her seat in the dining room. Her body vibrated and shivered, so hard that her muscles hurt. Fear and grief and memories pushed one sob and then another from her throat. She tried to breathe in and out slowly, but couldn't.

"This isn't Cody," she said, her voice choked with tears. "This is Seth, and he's okay. He's okay. He's okay." Maybe if she repeated it enough, she'd be able to pull herself to the present. "Seth is on the phone. He's okay."

"Olivia? What's wrong?" Samantha kneeled in front of her. "Honey, what do you need? What happened?"

"It's Seth. Not Cody. And Seth is okay," she blubbered. "Thank God. Seth is okay."

"I can't understand what you're saying." Samantha gently shook Olivia's shoulders. "Look at me. What do you need?"

Olivia raised her eyes to Samantha's. What did she need? "Grady. Get Grady." He, after all, was the only person in this house who would understand what she was feeling. Closing her eyes, she again tried to breathe slowly. In through her nose, out through her mouth, but all she saw were the police officers' faces at her door—how the snow had whipped in the air around them, landing on their jackets. How they'd hesitated before speaking. And then, all she heard were the words, "Your husband and son were involved in an automobile accident. Is there anyone we can call for you before we take you to the hospital?"

She'd had her freaking bathrobe on. She'd been drinking a glass of wine and reading a book, enjoying her precious time alone. When the doorbell rang, she hadn't even been afraid to answer it.

"Sweetheart, open your eyes." Grady's warm tenor wrapped around her. His thumbs found her cheeks, and he wiped her tears from beneath her eyes. "I'm here, baby. That was Seth on the phone. There's nothing to be upset about."

"Seth is okay," she whispered. She was cold. So cold. Her teeth started chattering as her shivers increased. "I thought…"

"I know what you thought. But he's fine. I promise." Grady rubbed her arms briskly. "Why did you think he wasn't? Sweetheart, they send someone to the house with bad news. It wouldn't come in the form of a phone call."

Right. She knew that. Of course, she knew that. How had she forgotten?

Grady continued talking in a soft, reassuring voice. "That's why Mom was so upset we didn't answer the door this morning. She gets a little freaked whenever the doorbell rings."

Okay. That made sense. Her brain understood. Why, then, couldn't she get those policemen's voices out of her head? "I c-can't breathe. Can't g-get away from that night."

"I'm here, baby. Right here. I want you to think about

something good. Anything at all that comes to mind. Can you do that for me?"

"Yes. The d-day Cody was b-born." She shivered again and wrapped her arms around herself, but kept her eyes glued shut. "Th-that is a good memory."

"You couldn't have chosen a better one, baby." Then, to someone else, Grady said, "She's freezing. Can we get her a blanket? And maybe something warm to drink?"

"I'll brew some tea," Karen said. "John, run upstairs and get a blanket from the linen closet. Jace? Turn the thermostat up a few degrees. And Samantha, maybe—"

"I'll stay with Olivia," Samantha said, giving no room for argument.

"See, Olly? We're all here. Everyone is okay," Grady said quietly.

She heard the worry in his voice, and she hated that she—once again—had caused him concern. But right now, she was marveling at the memory of her infant son. And oh, that was so much better than what was in her head a second ago.

"How's that memory going?" Grady asked. "Feeling any better yet?"

"He was so tiny and perfect. And his eyes...remember how blue they were when he was first born? I was sure they'd stay blue." Slowly, so very slowly, the greater edge of her panic began to recede. "And how he'd turn his head toward you whenever you'd talk? All those nights of reading to my belly did the trick, Grady. He loved your voice."

"I remember his cry. He sounded more like a baby kitten than a baby human for the first several weeks." Grady laughed at the memory. "But it wasn't too long before that changed. Man, he had some lungs on him."

Finally, the pressure on her chest and the sickening swirl in her stomach lightened. Joy filled her heart instead of panic. "I remember," she said as a blanket fell around her shoulders. "He liked to be heard."

"Just like my boys," Karen said from somewhere in front of Olivia. "Here's your tea, honey." She pushed the mug into Olivia's hand. "Drink some. It will warm your body and soothe your soul."

"Do you know what I remember?" Samantha asked, gripping Olivia's free hand. "How he'd startle whenever a loud truck passed outside your house, Olivia. Just like—"

"He did when I was still pregnant," Olivia filled in. Now, she laughed. "That's right. I'd forgotten all about that!"

John coughed as if to clear his throat. "Personally, I enjoyed how I was able to get him to fall asleep easier than anyone else. That little guy would curl up on my shoulder and in no time at all he'd be out. Made me feel good."

"And how his tiny fist would grab on to anything and tug," Jace said wistfully. "He used to pull my hair, my nose…"

Olivia opened her eyes. Grady was kneeling in front of her, watching her intently with a sweet smile on his face and concern in his eyes. Samantha was sitting in the chair to the right of her, Jace to the left. John and Karen were standing behind Grady.

They'd surrounded her. All of them. With love. With compassion. And they'd happily joined in to share memories of the child they'd all loved…had all lost. The child they all missed.

Letting go of Samantha's hand, Olivia reached hers out to Karen. Her mother-in-law grasped it instantly. "How are you feeling, honey?" Karen asked.

"I'm so very glad that Seth is okay," Olivia said, her voice thick with emotion. "And I am so sorry if my emotional craziness hurt the wonder of that phone call in any way. Please forgive me. I don't know what happened. I just…was so afraid you were hearing bad news. I couldn't bear it. And that, I guess—"

"You thought I was in pain and that brought you back to your pain. I know, dear." Karen's eyes shimmered with tears. "I understand, and I love you all the more for it."

"I'm glad Seth is okay," Olivia repeated. "That's what is important here. Not my meltdown."

"We're all important," Karen said sternly. But her gaze held warmth and love. Kindness and acceptance. "We're family. And this family sticks together. No matter what."

"Amen to that," John said. "Now, you're not going home tonight. You'll stay here, where we can look after you."

Her initial instinct was to politely say no, that it would be better for her to go home. The words were on the tip of her tongue when her heart stopped her. This Thanksgiving was nothing like the last one she'd spent in this house. It hadn't been a perfect day. Cody's boisterous laugh hadn't echoed through the rooms. The hours hadn't passed in easy comfort with her husband by her side. But she couldn't deny that one thing remained the same. One thing she couldn't have predicted. These people were her family. Despite everything that had happened. Despite everything she had done to try to prove otherwise.

Olivia drew in a deep breath and looked at Grady. He was a rock, steady and sure, and had stood by her side for so long. Was she ready to consider that maybe he had been right about them all along? She didn't know. But maybe she was finally willing to find out.

"Yes," she said quickly, before her fears rendered her speechless. "Being with my family is exactly what I need."

Chapter Eight

Olivia stared at the four large storage boxes of Christmas decorations she'd dragged up from the basement that morning. She'd yet to find the courage to actually open one of them, but they were cluttering up her living room all the same. And the dust! She should have wiped the boxes down before bringing them upstairs. Unfortunately, she hadn't exactly thought this out.

Her nose tickled with the beginnings of a sneeze. She pressed the bridge of her nose until the sensation disappeared. "So, are you going to decorate, or ogle the dang boxes?" she said into the empty room. Even her cat was avoiding her. Jasper, in his feline wisdom, had hidden himself somewhere the second he'd heard the commotion on the basement stairs.

Backing up, she sat on the edge of the sofa. "Quit mocking me," she said to the container nearest her. "I can do this. I got through Thanksgiving, didn't I? I can decorate."

128 MIRACLE UNDER THE MISTLETOE

Except... Well, maybe she couldn't. Dumb. So dumb to
think she could. In addition to stockings and lights, Santa
figurines and angels, those boxes held handmade ornaments from Cody. Some were made of paper and glitter,
others of popsicle sticks and paint, there were even a few
foam balls with sparkly sequins glued in haphazard pat-
terns. She remembered every one they'd ever made together, and those he'd made at preschool and—that last
year—in kindergarten.

There was also a "baby's first Christmas" ornament.
Two, actually. Plus the many, many other decorations that
she and Grady had accumulated over the years. Every
one of them told a story. Every one of them was bound to
break her heart.

"There isn't any harm in putting the boxes back down-
stairs," she whispered. "No one but you will know you
even tried. There's always next year. If you can't do this,
don't."

Standing, she paced the narrow path in between the
boxes. Thanksgiving had forced her to be honest with herself about a few things. For one, she went a little crazy at
John and Karen's house. Okay, a lot crazy. She'd had a few
panic attacks since Cody's death, but none of them quite
as bad as her Thanksgiving Day freak-out. And, frankly,
they weren't fun. She needed to find a way to learn how
to handle them.

Secondly, she discovered that it was possible to feel
good—happy, even—when she thought of Cody. How
precious and blissful those memories could be. She
really, really wanted to be able to get to that place without breaking down first. Decorating the house for Christmas seemed like a positive step forward. A way to find
the joy she felt at her in-laws' house three days ago. But
now, it seemed overwhelming. And a bad, bad idea.

"Crap," she muttered. "Take it all back down or grow a spine?" She crouched down and pulled the dusty lid off of one of the boxes. Inside were other containers, all carefully packed away. Jace and Seth had done that, she recalled, about a month after Cody's funeral. One day, Grady had taken her out, and when they'd come home, all of the Christmas stuff was gone. Poof. As if it had never existed.

She'd been furious that Grady would take it upon himself to have his brothers come in to their home and put everything away. Strange. Then, she wanted the house to look exactly the same as when Cody had last been here. And since then, she'd cleared away every physical reminder of Cody. Those items that had belonged to him, she'd tucked into his bedroom. Other items went into storage, others still went to Goodwill, and a few were thrown away.

"I'm not going to do this," she whispered. Resolutely she replaced the lid and stood. "Not without your father, Cody. He should be here for this."

Yes. That was the right decision. Before she found a million and one reasons not to, she picked up her phone and called him. He answered on the second ring. "Grady, I need your help," she said. "Could you please come over here?"

"Are you all right?"

"Yes. But there is something I want to do." Her voice was soft, hesitant. "Something I need to do. But it doesn't feel right without you here." Now, her voice hitched. A frisson of strength straightened her backbone. She took in a breath and continued, "I think you'll want to be here for this. I hope so, anyway."

He was quiet for long enough that she began to worry, but then, "I'm on my way."

While she waited, she brewed a pot of coffee. She was carrying her filled-to-the-brim cup through the hallway when she saw her reflection in a mirror. Her hair was still damp from her morning shower, so it hung limply around her face. Naturally, she didn't have any makeup on because what woman in their right mind slathered on cosmetics when alone on a Sunday? None that she knew. The area beneath her eyes was dark enough to appear bruised, and her skin... Well, John was right. She was definitely on the pale side. Almost sickly so.

As if waking up from a dreamless sleep, she noticed the waistband of her jeans was loose and her sweater seemed a full size too large. Had she lost weight? When? Deep in thought, she took the stairs to her bedroom and somehow managed not to spill coffee all over the place. Once there, she set her cup down and stripped off her clothes.

"Honesty time," she murmured, stepping in front of her full-length mirror. The first thing she noticed was that she had, indeed, lost weight. Not enough to cause alarm, especially because she probably could've stood to drop a few pounds to begin with. After Cody was born, an extra ten pounds or so had stuck to her frame relentlessly.

The second thing she noticed about her body was its lack of muscle tone. Well, duh. While she'd never been a go-to-the-gym sort of girl, she had lived a fairly active life. *Before.* The most activity she got now was walking up and down the stairs in her house. Heck, most days, she was exhausted by the time she sat down at her desk at work.

She looked weak and insubstantial. Not to mention, sad and listless. In truth, she didn't recognize the woman looking out at her from the mirror. Feeling very much as if she'd been doused by a bucket of icy water, she put her clothes back on. If she really wanted to focus on the future, then she needed to start making changes in her present.

Beginning now.

Grady stuck his keys in his pocket and knocked on Olivia's door. He couldn't get over that she'd called him, let alone that she'd asked him to come over. He'd hoped that the softening in her eyes on Thanksgiving hadn't been his imagination playing tricks. And when she'd said that she wanted to be with her family, he prayed that statement included him.

A minute passed without Olivia letting him in, so he knocked again. That was when he noticed the music. Christmas carols? The invisible noose that had increasingly tightened around his heart loosened up a notch. He twisted the doorknob to see if she'd left the door unlocked. She had. He pushed it open and the sounds of Dean Martin singing "Winter Wonderland" filled his ears. Now, his heart did a rat-a-tat-tat series of thumps.

This house had been his home for so long. The place he returned to his family after a long day at work. Where he'd painted the walls, fixed creaky pipes, laughed with his wife and sat by his son's bed to read him a story. He knew every nook and cranny of the place. And whether he lived here or not, this was home.

"Olivia?" he called. "I'm here!" He walked in, removed his coat and slung it over the stair banister on his way into the living room.

She sat on the floor in the middle of a group of large, plastic storage containers. The lids were off two of them, and several smaller containers were open—their contents spilled in a half circle around Olly's feet. She was holding an ornament in one hand—a pint-size, glued-together popsicle-stick picture frame—and tears were streaming down her cheeks before dripping off her chin. His throat seemed to close in emotion, in worry and in wonder.

He approached her slowly, not wanting to startle her. "Sweetheart?" She continued to stare at the ornament Cody had made for her the Christmas before the accident. The picture in the frame was of a four-year-old Cody building a snowman in their front yard. Grady had helped cut the picture down in size so it would fit. "So, what do we have going on here?" he asked.

She gave no sign of being aware of his presence. Bending at the knees, Grady shoved one of the unopened boxes to the side, and then sat down cross-legged in front of his wife. An internal debate raged: Try to get her attention, or simply sit and wait? "Winter Wonderland" faded away, replaced by "Let it Snow, Let it Snow, Let it Snow." Next, he knew, was "Silent Night." This was Olly's favorite Christmas CD. She loved Dean Martin.

"You always played this CD when we baked cookies," he said, keeping his voice low and steady. "Also when we decorated. It's nice to hear Dean again, Olly."

Again, no response. He moved the pile of ornaments to the side and shifted his body so he was seated next to her. Grady gently touched Cody's picture. In a split-second, that day replayed itself in Grady's mind. "He was so serious about that snowman. The snowballs had to be the perfect shape, and it took him forever to decide which of my scarves should go around the snowman's neck."

"Yes. We had to go to the store, because Cody needed the perfect carrot for the nose." Olivia wiped the wetness from her cheeks, but kept her gaze on their son. "The ones we had in the house weren't long enough. And the eyes! They had to be just like Frosty's, but we didn't have any coal." Her body rippled with a slight laugh. "So we painted a couple of rocks black."

"And we never did find a corncob pipe," Grady remembered. Pressure gathered behind his eyes. "He was some kid, wasn't he? We were extraordinarily lucky to have him in our lives."

Olivia inhaled a shaky breath. Carefully, as if it were made of porcelain, she set the ornament down. She looked at Grady with a small, tremulous smile. "I want to decorate for Christmas. Today. Will you help me?"

Such a simple request. People filled their homes with Christmas cheer every year without thought. But this request from Olivia was about far more than putting up twinkle lights or hanging stockings from the fireplace. She was bringing warmth and love, and in her way, Cody, back into her home. Into her life. And she'd asked him to help.

"I would love nothing better," he said.

"Thank you." Her smile grew a little wider. "And don't worry. We're still set for next weekend. I'm not asking for this to be our third date or anything."

"I didn't think you were." The mention of date number three made his insides twist. Well, he could always change his mind, depending on how today went. Maybe they wouldn't need date three. Maybe they'd be able to speed ahead to date four. "But before we can do any decorating, we'll need to buy you a Christmas tree."

"Oh!" She glanced around the room. "I guess that would be helpful, wouldn't it? I'd want a real tree, like always. Do you think it's too early to get one and have it last through Christmas Day?"

"I think we can manage it. If not, we buy another in mid-December. Whatever will keep you smiling." He meant it, too. If necessary, he'd buy her a tree every week between now and Christmas, and decorate them all. "I like seeing you smile, Olly."

She wiped her cheeks again. "You know what? It feels good to want to smile." Standing up, she brushed dust off of her jeans. "Okay. Let's do it. I want a huge, beautiful tree, Grady. It has to be perfect. For Cody."

By silent agreement, they went to Sauvie Island Farms in search of the perfect tree. Being there wasn't easy for Olivia. After all, they'd gone there as a family for hayrides and pumpkins every Halloween, and for wreathes and trees every Christmas. The farm used to have music in the trees, choirs playing Christmas carols and booths selling deliciously rich hot chocolate.

Most of these little extras seemed to be gone—or perhaps it was just too early in the season—but that didn't change the fact that everything she saw, every scent in the air, was another memory.

What really got to her was the other families. Husbands and wives and children joyfully chattering and laughing as they searched for the tree that would sit in their homes for the next month. She was ashamed to admit that she was jealous of these families. She nearly turned around and headed for the truck, but Grady had clasped her hand in his and pulled her to his side.

Somehow, that bolstered her courage enough that she was able to force her legs to walk. She recognized Cody's tree the second she saw it. An absolutely gorgeous Douglas fir that stood eight feet tall, had beautiful branches filled with fresh, fragrant needles and was likely a good five or six feet in diameter. Cody would've jumped up and down in excitement over it.

Now, they were back at Olivia's house and it was almost time for the real work to begin. She had Dean Martin singing, a huge bowl of popcorn buttered and salted and two steaming mugs of hot cocoa with extra marsh-mallows.

"You always had a knack for choosing great trees," Grady said, after lugging the massive pine in the house and putting it in its stand. "I think this might be the best one yet."

"I don't know about that, but she's certainly a beauty." Olivia held out his mug of cocoa. "Here. I added a little vanilla to the mix, and I popped some popcorn."

He laughed in a small, almost tentative way. "Just like the old days." He accepted the cup, drank some and gestured toward the boxed-up decorations. "So, which of these do you think is hiding the Christmas lights?"

"I don't have a clue. But I guess we should find out." She cleared a space in the middle of the containers and sat down. Patting the floor, she said, "Come on, let's do this."

He moved toward her and stopped. "Are you sure you're up for this, Olly?" He swallowed another gulp of his hot chocolate. "This is a lot to deal with in one day. We could take a break and finish later. Or tomorrow night. Whenever you're ready."

"I'm ready now." Okay, sort of a lie. But waiting wouldn't help her get any more ready, now would it? Besides, "If we put this off, the mess in here will drive me nuts. I'll likely end up decorating, anyway. I'd rather do this with you, Grady."

"Right. I get that." He sat down a few feet from her and set his mug on the floor beside him. "It's just that I—" Tension laced his words. "Never mind, Olly. Now is fine."

Oh, jeez. Maybe *he* needed a break? This had to be difficult for him, too. Once again, her blindness to Grady's needs smacked her across the forehead. "Hey," she said softly, "Are you okay? If you'd rather hold off, we can do that."

"I'm a little off balance," he admitted in a strained voice. "I...I haven't seen any of these decorations since—" He clamped his jaw shut and looked somewhere off to her right. "This might be rough."

For so long, Grady had only shown her his strong, noble side. He was always there, ready to help her, to protect her, to do whatever it was she said she needed. Now, in this moment, it was her turn to be strong. It was her turn to protect.

"We'll wait then," she said decisively. Reaching over, she lightly rested her hand on his knee. "You're right, Grady. We don't have to do this now. I should have realized that this would be just as difficult for you as it is for me. I'm sorry."

His leg tensed beneath her palm. When he looked at her, there were shadows in his eyes. "It isn't so much that I want to wait," he said carefully, as if choosing the right words were of the utmost importance. "I'm worried that my emotions will get the better of me. That I'll react in a way that might upset you more." The muscle in his cheek flinched. "You're trying so hard here, sweetheart. What if I make it worse for you?"

She couldn't speak. Even now, Grady's concern for her overrode all else? He was worried about how *she* would be if he had a moment of sadness or pain? She had done this to him. She had made him feel as if he couldn't count on her. How had she been so blind for so long? He deserved so much more. So much better.

Shamed to the core of her being, she rolled forward to her knees and crawled over to sit next to him. Brushing her fingertips along the side of his face, she said, "I'll lean on you. You lean on me. How does that sound?"

Grady inhaled a long, slow breath. He placed his hand over hers and they laced their fingers together. She laid her head on his chest, and he rested his chin in her hair. Neither of them spoke for a long while. Dean Martin finished singing "White Christmas" and two other songs before they separated.

"So," Olivia said with a little cough. "Lights."

"Right." Grady reached for one of the boxes. "Let's find those lights."

He swiveled to the left, she swiveled to the right, and somehow, they ended up supporting each other back to back. The feel of his body pressed against hers was warm and reassuring and so very, very real. It—*he*—gave her strength. Was she doing the same for him? She hoped so.

They began sifting through containers in silence, searching for the oversize multicolored blinking lights Cody had insisted they buy. When Dean began his rendition of "Jingle Bells," she found herself singing along. Before too long, Grady joined in. Her lips stretched into a smile and she couldn't help but bop along with the music. Silly, maybe, but the movement and the singing energized her. Exhilarated her. She—believe it or not—felt *happy*.

Grady stopped singing midnote. "Aha!" he said brightly. "Found them."

And, just that fast, melancholy slipped in to replace the happiness. "In the very last box, of course," she said as she rose to a stand. Reaching out, she grasped on to him and tried to sound as bright as he. "Come on, old man, let's light up this room."

"Old? Old, you say?" Instead of standing, he pulled her into his lap. "Can an old man do that?"

She gave a little laugh. "Actually, yes. Doesn't take a lot of strength to tug someone into your arms."

"Hmm. Well, I suppose you have a point." And then he

looked at her. Really looked at her. Like all the way into her soul. "Have I told you lately how beautiful you are? I have thought so from the second we met, and my opinion has never changed."

Heat crept along her skin, from her toes to her ears and everywhere in between. "Then you must be old, because you're losing your eyesight. I'm…faded."

"No. You're radiant."

And there went her bones, melting into a big puddle. "Are you flirting with me?"

"Maybe," he said with a long-lashed wink. "Do you have a problem with that?"

"Umm…" Did she? "No, I don't think I do. I'm out of practice, I guess."

"I'm an amazing tutor. My advice is to set up some study sessions immediately. My calendar gets crowded fast," he teased while trailing his finger along the curve of her jaw. How could such a small, simple touch set her on fire? "We can start with corny pick-up lines."

"Such as?" she whispered. "Give me an example."

His lips twitched in an almost grin. "Do you have a Band-Aid?"

"Why? Did you scrape your knee falling for me?"

The grin became full-fledged. "I did. Over and over and over."

Oh. Her insides turned all soft and wiggly. "You're a dork."

"For you? Guilty as charged."

"Well, as sweet as this is…the lights aren't getting hung," she said breathlessly. How could this man, whom she'd known for so long, make her feel like a love-struck, silly teenager? Crazy. "And I believe I've proven we can skip the corny pick-up line lessons. I'm fairly well versed, after all."

"I don't know about those lights." Grady stroked the area underneath her eyes, apparently noticing her oh-so-attractive dark circles. She tried to pull back, but his other arm held her firm. "You must be tired, honey."

"Not really, just—"

"Because you've been running through my mind all day."

"What?"

"You know...running?" he said, deadpan. "Tired?"

"Oh!" Her entire body quaked with laughter. "I so didn't see that one coming. Nice one, Grady."

Excruciatingly slowly, as if nothing else in the universe mattered, as if no one else existed but for them, he pulled her to him tight and held her. Her head lay on his shoulder, and if she moved the tiniest bit, she'd be able to kiss his neck. And then, maybe she'd move on to his ear...his cheek...his jaw...his mouth. But she didn't move, even though her body cried out for her to. She barely breathed. This wasn't like the other hugs they'd shared, either before or after Cody. This embrace seemed to have a language that only they understood.

It was sweet and quiet and oh-so-intimate.

Holding each other seemed exactly right. Anything more would be too much. At least for now. At least for today. So she enjoyed the comfort of his arms around her and hers around him. She breathed in his scent, rubbed her cheek against the softness of his shirt and allowed herself to revel in the present. In *this* moment. On *this* day.

After a while, and she had no idea how much time had passed because Dean had long since stopped singing, they reluctantly separated and got to the business of decorating.

Naturally, they started with the lights. Surprisingly, they all functioned. Grady was taller, so he dealt with the top of the pine, and she fed him the strings of lights as necessary. Once they reached the middle of the tree, they took their positions on either side and worked together to weave the lights in and out of the branches.

Neither spoke until the tree held what seemed to be thousands of blinking lights. Olivia's heart squeezed as she looked over their handiwork. Yes, Cody would have been thrilled. He'd have asked Daddy to hold him up high so he could put decorations on the "toppest" part of the tree. Grady would've done so, and Olivia would've come up from behind and tickled Cody.

God. She could almost hear his squeals and his giggles. A sigh as heavy as an anchor expelled from her lungs. Her gaze met Grady's and she saw that he was battling with his own memories. Yep. This was hard. Really, really hard.

"Why don't we hang the basic stuff first?" Grady asked softly. "And set aside any of Cody's ornaments. It might be easier to put those on last, all at once. We can celebrate him then, Olly. Instead of breaking it up into tiny moments. What do you think?"

She almost lost it then. Because to her, there was nothing to celebrate here. This was about moving forward. This was about learning to experience the joy of her son in the present. "What an odd word to use," she whispered. "Celebrate what? Getting through Christmas without our son? Because I'm sure you didn't mean to say we should celebrate his death?"

"Of course not! Celebrate his *life*." He went to her and opened his arms. She stepped out of his reach. "Celebrate our love for him. That's all I meant to say."

She stared at Grady, once again questioning her motivation for doing this now. Why couldn't she be like her husband? Why couldn't she see moments like this as a cause for celebration instead of something she had to get through?

"I'm sorry I misunderstood," she said in a wobbly voice. "But I...I want to be able to understand, to see things as you do. I'm trying."

"I know."

"Do you care if I put the music on again?" she asked, fraught with the want to move on from this place. "It distracts me."

"Music is good," he said with a small smile.

So, with Dean singing his Christmas heart out, she pulled her courage together and helped Grady separate the boxes of ornaments. They zigzagged around the tree and each other while hanging the simpler, easier-to-manage Santa Clauses, snowmen and angels, along with a mixture of other Christmas curios they'd picked up over the years.

Every now and then, Grady would ask her if she was okay. In between those moments, she'd ask him how he was doing. And then, quicker than she'd have thought possible, there weren't any ornaments besides Cody's left.

Olivia's throat tightened as she searched the room, looking for anything—even a freaking candy cane—that would put off the inevitable. Other than the standard half dozen or so ornaments that had somehow broken since they were last used, there was nothing.

"Well. I guess that's it." She crossed over and picked up the box that held the decorations that reminded them of Cody. Some were crafted by him, some were his favorites, some were chosen by him at one time or another, and then there were those that had belonged to him. A myriad of memories bundled together in a plastic box. "How should we do this?"

"One at a time." Grady stood in front of her and reached

into the container. He pulled out a store-bought ornament of a miniature mouse holding a green-wrapped Hershey's Kiss. "Remind me," Grady said in a hushed tone. "When did Cody get this little guy?"

"Cody was four. The three of us were shopping for your family," she replied instantly. "And Cody saw the display of candy boxed with various ornaments. He thought...he thought it was funny that a mouse would want chocolate instead of cheese." She tipped her chin up hoping to stop the tears from falling. "I snuck that into the cart for his Christmas stocking."

"Ah," Grady said. "That's right. So, sweetheart, where should we hang this one?"

She attempted to answer, but her vocal cords refused to cooperate. Instead, she waved her hand in the general direction of the tree and shrugged.

"The front of the tree? Do you think the top or the bottom?"

She still couldn't answer—not without bawling, anyway—so she shrugged again and continued to stare at the ceiling.

"How about if I take care of Mr. Mouse here while you choose the next ornament?"

Okay. She could do that. She *wanted* to do that. Behind her, Grady hummed in tune to the Christmas music, apparently seeking out the ideal place for the mouse. She reached in and blindly grabbed an object. Then, without looking at what she held, she placed the box on the coffee table and turned to face the tree. Mr. Mouse was almost at the very top.

And her husband... Well, she couldn't see his face. But he stood so straight and so tall and so motionless that she knew he was fighting to control his emotions. Somehow, in a way she didn't understand, that pushed her forward.

She closed the gap between them and oh-so-gently ran her hand down his sweater-covered back. His muscles jerked in response.

"You found the perfect spot," she said. "A place of honor for one of Cody's favorite decorations."

A minute passed before Grady answered. When he did, she heard nothing but calmness and clarity in his tenor. "Well, come on, Olly. Mr. Mouse deserves nothing less. Besides, I figured he's so small that he'd appreciate being up so high."

"Cody logic."

"Yup." Pivoting, he asked, "Did you choose one?"

"I did." She held up her hand, showing him the ornament. A ceramic candy cane that Cody had painted in bold splashes of red and green. "He brought this home from kindergarten his last day before Christmas break. He ran into the house and straight to the tree. He hung it—" she stepped to the side of Grady, crouched, and slipped the hook over a bottom branch "—right about here."

When she stood, Grady was ready with the next ornament. From there on out, they took turns in selecting, reminiscing and decorating. Instead of becoming easier, as she'd hoped, the task only grew harder as they continued on. Which, she supposed, made sense, considering the circumstances. Strangely, though, as difficult as the process was, she still felt a lightening of the spirit. And in a way that she couldn't begin to explain, she felt physically closer to her son. His presence was so strong, she kept expecting to hear his voice or see his smile.

"There," Grady said after placing the last ornament— the popsicle-stick picture frame with the photo of Cody— on the tree. This one Grady had put in the front and center position, with all the other ornaments framing Cody.

"So beautiful," she whispered. "Truly."

Again, her husband stood straight and tall, his attention on the tree...on their son. Emotion welled in her chest, and she—again—stepped forward to place her hand on her husband's back. A deep, almost guttural sob choked out of Grady's throat. She pressed her forehead against his shoulder and let the tears she'd held flow.

Grady turned and captured her in his arms. Dean was crooning "Silent Night" in only the way that Dean could. Olivia had always loved the quiet beauty of the song, but never so much as she did at that minute. Every word resonated in her heart and soul. She raised her arms and wrapped them around Grady's neck.

And then, in silent celebration of their son, they danced.

Chapter Nine

The next week passed in a blur. Each morning, Olivia would take a few minutes before leaving for work to stand in front of the Christmas tree. And each evening, she curled herself on the sofa—sometimes with a book, sometimes not—and let the blinking lights do their magic. The icy frost she'd shielded her heart with for the past three years was slowly melting.

It was scary and wondrous, all at once.

As the deep freeze let go of its hold, she began to notice little things in her world. Like the way her next-door neighbors—an elderly couple who'd been together for so long they resembled each other—would stop and wave whenever they saw her. Had they always done that? Had she ever waved back? She didn't know.

Then, one night when she dashed into the grocery store to pick up something for dinner, she was startled when the cashier greeted her by name. The woman also asked after Olivia's cat and wished her a Merry Christmas. Try as she might, she couldn't remember ever speaking with the cashier before, when obviously she had.

And here at work, she was blindsided to see how her co-workers, while always kind and polite, kept their distance unless there was something job-related they required from her. Yet, they spoke easily and often with each other. Apparently, in the two-plus years Olivia had been employed here, she hadn't gone out of her way to get to know anyone.

She, like the Dickens' character, had closed her eyes to the people in her life. Not out of monetary greed, but out of self-preservation. But really, was that any better? She'd still become indifferent—cold—to everyone and everything. Well, except for Samantha. Even with her, though, Olivia recognized that she had put limitations on their friendship.

All of this needed to change. So, she did something she probably should have done years ago—she made an appointment with a grief counselor before she lost her nerve. She... Well, she was ready to fully wake up. But she needed to do so on her terms and in her way. That was why she chose to keep this decision to herself. At least for now.

Ugh. Shoving herself away from her desk, she grabbed a sheaf of papers and headed for the copy machine. Thank God it was Friday. There were two hours left before the workday ended, and while she'd managed to mostly catch up on her workload, staying focused had proved to be an issue. How could it not with everything that was going on inside of her?

She punched the required number of copies into the machine and hit the start button. The swish-swish of the papers sifting through the cycle silenced the background noise of patients chatting in the waiting room, which was just on the other side of the door.

Her mind wandered while she waited, once again going to Sunday. Decorating the tree with Grady had been tough. Okay, huge understatement. Sunday's activities had left her raw. But a sweetness existed there, as well. A sweetness she couldn't have experienced with anyone other than her husband.

Her husband. She'd been thinking a lot about that, too. About what he wanted. About what she wanted. She'd known for a long time that she'd never be whole without Cody, but she was beginning to sense that expunging Grady from her life would only increase her emptiness. But was that a good enough reason to stay in their marriage? Especially when she wasn't sure if she was capable of giving him what he needed.

Hell, she didn't know. But she loved him, and she believed he loved her. It was the what-ifs that were killing her. What if she let him down? What if, once he understood that she blamed herself for the car accident, he blamed her, too? What if he couldn't forgive her? What if she could never tell him? And the kicker: What if they reconciled, found their way to happiness again, only to face another tragedy down the line?

So many what-ifs. She yearned for a guaranteed happily-ever-after. A promise that the rest of her life would only be filled with joy. Since that was impossible for anyone who lived outside of a novel, she had to decide if the risk of losing everything—again—was worth it.

And that decision needed to be made soon.

Grady held the bucket of popcorn out for Olivia. She grinned, scooped a handful and returned her attention to the screen. They were seated in a darkened theater watching a movie. A romantic comedy, no less. Grady had chosen this particular movie on purpose, but Olivia hadn't caught on yet. Well, to be honest, why would she? They'd seen hundreds of movies together, and a fair number of them were romantic comedies.

Grady had taken Olivia to such a movie about ten months after Cody's funeral. Getting her out of the house back then had been nearly impossible, but he had to do something. He was hopeless with grief, with loneliness, and he saw her spiraling away from him. Each day, she closed herself off more and more, and each day grew bleaker. He'd asked her to go see a therapist with him. She refused. So he went on his own. The therapist had suggested changing their daily routine to draw her out. It had taken weeks to get Olivia to agree to an outing.

There hadn't been a must-see action movie playing at the time, which would have been his first pick. His choices had been a romantic comedy, a tear-jerker of a drama, a horror flick and a few family-friendly films. Obviously, given those choices, he'd gone with the romantic comedy. Even so, unless she somehow narrowed in on that day, the chances were high she wouldn't connect this movie to the one they saw that afternoon. Nope. It would be their next stop that would clue her in.

Chances were, all hell would break loose then.

Fidgeting in his seat, he stretched his legs out. Olivia and the rest of the audience laughed at something the dashing hero said to the wistful heroine, but Grady didn't know what. He couldn't concentrate. He'd fought with himself all week about today's date. Here they were, and he still hadn't decided if his plan would prove beneficial.

Or, hell, if he should even follow through.

Sure, Olivia had handled Sunday well enough. In some respects, better than he. But tonight was a beast of a different variety. And damn, he ached to protect her from every ill the world might throw her way. Naturally, he knew he couldn't, which only served to make him feel worse about the hours ahead.

But…he'd set up these dates for a reason. They were meant to serve a purpose. With date one, his goal was to remind Olivia of who they were before Cody, of the early nuances of their relationship. Thanksgiving… Okay, he'd taken a misstep, there. A stupid one. He'd initially introduced Olivia to his family on Thanksgiving Day, about seven months into their courtship. That was what he'd hoped she'd connect with, and therefore, reconnect with his family. But he should've realized that the underlying tension over Seth could affect her, and he damn well should have known she'd be more likely to think of the last Thanksgiving they'd celebrated together as a family. So yes. A huge misstep.

Fortunately for him, the day hadn't completely bottomed out. Whatever she'd felt at his parents' had paved the way for what had taken place last Sunday. Even with all the emotional ups and downs, he considered every second of that day a gift. He was pretty sure that Olly would say the same. A breath he hadn't realized he'd been holding wheezed from his chest, and some of his anxiety eased off. Perhaps date three would also turn into a gift.

The audience laughed again, startling him enough that his arm jerked and a good portion of the popcorn dumped into his lap. "Damn it," he muttered.

"Are you okay?" Olivia asked. She leaned over to help him clean up the mess. "You don't seem as if you're having a very good time."

"I'm fine," he assured her. "And I'm with the most beautiful woman here, so how could I not be having a good time?"

"Hmm," she said with a grin. "That sounds suspiciously like a corny pick-up line."

"Nothing corny about it, darlin'," he said, tossing a piece of popcorn into his mouth. "The movie's great. Even better than I heard."

"Sure it is," she drawled. "I can see that you're absolutely riveted."

"Shh," he said. "I'm trying to pay attention here."

Olivia narrowed her eyes in doubt, but didn't press the issue. Once she was engaged in the movie again, Grady returned to his musings. Tonight's date—date number three—was all about dragging the dirty laundry out. He felt sure she blamed him for the accident. He felt just as sure that she needed to find the courage to tell him so. Whether she screamed, hollered or threw things at him, he didn't care. He was ready for it. Beyond that, they had never really talked about what had happened that night. The air had never been cleared.

It wasn't as if he hadn't tried, but Olivia always shut him down. Now, he understood that they had to have this conversation. That if they didn't expose the raw underside of their pain, of their worst fears, they would never be able to move beyond it—whether separately or together. So yeah, as fervently as he wished otherwise, as much as he questioned this path he'd chosen, somehow he was going to have to find a way to help Olly feel secure enough to speak her mind.

That didn't mean he was looking forward to it. If Olivia retreated into herself again, he wasn't sure he had the strength to continue his efforts. A man could only fight for so long. But if they got through tonight, then maybe they'd get through tomorrow, and the next day, and so on.

Olly, as if she knew his thoughts were on her, took the bucket of popcorn and set it on the ground. Then, she slipped her hand in his and rested her cheek on his shoulder. The tropical scent of her hair reached his nose. He almost asked her why she was using a different shampoo, but stopped himself. Sammy was right...what did it matter?

Enough brooding, he thought. He hadn't lied. He was with the most beautiful woman in the theater—and no, he didn't have to see all the other women to know that.

He only had eyes for Olivia.

Wrapping his arm around Olivia's shoulders, he pulled her closer to him. She sighed and snuggled in. With great effort, he forced himself to watch the movie. Stage two of their date would come soon enough. And then he'd see what he—they—had left.

"I don't want to be here," Olivia said in a tense whisper that matched the set of her shoulders. "Please take me home, Grady."

"I can't do that," he answered stiffly. "Not yet."

"Something like this isn't up to you, Grady. You don't get to make these decisions for me," Olivia snapped, annoyed beyond belief that he would try this again. "And I am not prepared to join a parents' bereavement group. Not when you dragged me here before and not now."

"You don't have to join. You never have to come back again." Grady tightened his grip on the steering wheel and stared at the building they were parked in front of. "All we have to do is go in and sit down and listen. That's it. I'll be with you the entire time."

"How could you plan this as our *date?*" It was on the tip of her tongue to confess she'd made an appointment with a counselor, but she didn't. Mostly because he wouldn't understand why she was willing to do that and not this. "Take me home, or I'll get out and call for a cab."

"You won't even try?" he asked in a deadly calm manner.

"You cannot continue to push me into situations I don't want to be in." She smacked her palm against the dashboard to punctuate her statement, her anger. "So no, Grady. For this...I won't even try."

He sighed, put the truck in Reverse, and backed out of the parking space. "After last weekend, I thought you might be ready for this."

"You thought wrong." Yes, she treasured what had taken place last weekend. Had even grown from it. But, "Decorating the house was *my* decision. My choice. This isn't."

"This group has helped me a lot."

"Good for you."

"They could help you, too," he said stubbornly.

Right. As if sitting in a circle of people sharing their horror stories would help her feel better about her own. She was too private for that. One-on-one with a therapist would be difficult enough, but she was ready to take that step. Talking about her feelings, about Cody, in a group?

No. That wasn't for her.

"They helped you, and that's great. I really mean that, Grady. But when are you going to understand that we are two different people? You had no right to bring me here." Another smack against the dashboard. Crap, that one stung. "You didn't even ask!"

"Because you would've said no. I thought, maybe, when presented with the opportunity, you would take a chance in trusting me."

Damn it! Why couldn't he understand? "This isn't about trust."

"I didn't make you go in, did I?" He slowed to a stop at a streetlight. "I hoped you would, yes. But I wouldn't force you into this, Olly. Hell, I would never force you into anything."

"Wow. What a short memory you have. Why are we even on this *date,* Grady?"

"Okay, I take that back. In all of the years that we've known each other, I've forced you into something once." The light turned green. He eased on the gas. "And yeah, I'll admit it was wrong. And probably a stupid idea. But I'm trying to save our marriage and I was desperate."

Her throat closed, and she knew if she tried to speak again, her voice would break. She didn't want to feel vulnerable. She wanted to feel mad, so she kept her mouth shut.

Twenty-five minutes later, they arrived at her house. Her temper had faded into a frantic desire to be alone. She opened the door and nearly leapt from the truck the second it stopped. Grady's long legs caught up with her before she'd even pulled her key from her purse.

"Invite me in, Olly," he said brusquely, although not unkindly. "We need to talk."

She jerked her shoulders back and tried to find her anger from earlier. "And if I say no? Will you demand to come in anyway?"

Resigned weariness dropped over his features. "No. I'll leave if you want." He pulled his keys out of his pocket and tugged the house key off of the ring. Offering it to her, he said, "Here. You deserve to know that when you lock your doors, no one else will come in. I should've returned this to you a long time ago."

She stared at the key but didn't move to take it. "Why now?"

He looked at her for so long, she thought he wasn't going to answer. When he did, his voice sounded hollow and far, far away. "Because I'm tired of this, Olly."

She swallowed heavily, feeling as if a stone was lodged in her windpipe. "Tired of what?"

"Trying to figure out how to help you." He pressed the key into her hand. "I don't know what you need. I keep thinking I do, but I'm wrong at every turn. And hell, every last thing I've tried has backfired."

Olivia recognized that she stood on a precipice. She wasn't prepared to make a decision this second about Grady, about their marriage. But if she entered her house and closed the door between them, then he would leave. And perhaps he wouldn't return. Her fist wrapped around Grady's key, the feel of it cold and heavy and hard.

Casting her eyes to the ground, she said, "What do we need to talk about?"

"What don't we need to talk about?" was his gruff response.

Well, that was about as clear as mud. But also entirely accurate. Using Grady's key, she unlocked the door. "Then I suppose we should get started."

He followed her in. She paused for a millisecond at the threshold to the living room before going to the kitchen. Shrugging off her coat, she draped it over the back of a chair. "Do you want anything to drink? I have a few beers. A bottle of wine. Coffee."

"Whatever you're having." After removing his coat, Grady sat at the table.

She poured each of them a glass of wine and slipped into the chair across from him. Angling her arms across her chest, she said, "Go for it."

He tapped his fingers against the table. What seemed an endlessly long minute passed. Finally, he said, "I don't know where to begin." Now, he gripped his hand into a fist. "That's not true. I know where to begin. I know exactly what to say. I'm just not sure how much you'll let me get out."

A strong, sharp jab of intuition sped her pulse. Ice trickled down her spine. Her tongue felt as if it were slicked with something sticky…like honey or peanut butter or maple syrup. Instead of leaving or asking Grady to leave, as her instincts begged her to do, she downed a large mouthful of wine. "Go for it," she repeated thickly. "Say what you need to say and I'll do my best to listen."

Closing his eyes, Grady leaned backward in his chair and expelled a breath. "The mall was crazy that day. The Christmas music was loud, but not loud enough to drown out all the folks trying to get their shopping done. Every time Cody spoke, I had to bend down to his level in order to hear him." A rough laugh emerged. "And the line for Santa was beyond nuts. We waited for over an hour before it was Cody's turn."

Olivia drained the rest of her wine and poured herself another glass. It was as if her heart had split into two. One half desperately needed to hear what Grady was saying. The other half craved to return to the protective cocoon she'd spent so long building.

"But the wait was worth it," Grady continued, "and Cody was all lit up from the inside after seeing Santa. When we left the mall, the parking lot was a slushy mess and the snow was still falling pretty hard. I was afraid Cody would slip, so I picked him up to carry him to the car." Here, Grady's voice deepened and cracked. "I thought about taking him back inside to wait out the snow. I almost did."

Whoa. Olivia hadn't known that. Wasn't sure she wanted to know it now. "Oh, God," she whispered. "You mean—"

Opening his eyes, Grady nodded. Misery clouded his

gaze. "Yeah. That's what I mean, Olly. If I'd only paused long enough to let that idea take hold…."

"The accident might never have happened," she filled in, her throat now dry instead of sticky. Yes. The what-ifs were surely going to kill her. "You've carried this around with you for all this time?"

"Yes." Grady's jaw hardened. "I wish to God I'd taken Cody back inside and bought him a cookie or…"

"Why didn't you?"

"It was two days before Christmas. I wanted all of us to be together. I…I thought I'd be able to get us home safely." Grief thinned his face, paled his normally tawny complexion to an ashen gray. "I was wrong. And that… that decision haunts me."

She understood being haunted by a split-second decision. All too well, even. "The accident wasn't your fault."

"I thought it was for a long time." He paused, as if deliberating what to say next. Or, more likely, *how.* "Even now, there are moments where I have to remind myself of that. And I would understand," he said slowly, "if you blamed me. I wouldn't be angry about it, Olly. Our son was in my care and I didn't bring him home. I *should* have brought him home."

"I don't blame you," she said, matching his slow, methodical beat. This was important. He *needed* to believe her. "I never have. I've told you this before, Grady. There are a lot of things I've done wrong since Cody died, but I have never lied to you about this." Reaching over, she grasped his wrist. "I do not blame you."

Their eyes met. She held his gaze with hers steadily, wanting him to see she spoke only the truth. A shudder rippled through his body. He shook his head back and forth in a physical denial of her assurances. "If that's true," he said, "then I don't understand."

"Understand what?"

"Why you've looked at me with such…coldness for so long." He stood and paced the kitchen like a pent-up wild animal locked inside of a cage. "Why you pushed me away along with everyone else. We were partners. In this life together, come good or bad. But I…we…lost Cody, and then I lost you, too. I want to know *why*."

"I don't know! I'm still trying to figure a lot of this out. But—" A desperate swirl of emotions engulfed her. She wasn't ready for this conversation. Yet ready or not, the time had come. He needed to hear the truth. Hell, maybe she needed to speak it.

"How can I blame you when I blame myself?" And then, before her nerves evaporated in a puff of smoke, she pushed out the rest, "It is *my* fault that you and Cody were even in the car that day. My fault, Grady. Not yours."

The shock of her words hit him first. She saw that by the way his entire body stilled and tensed. Disbelief came next, as evidenced by the ragged shaking of his head, by the slouch of his shoulders, by the way his eyebrows bunched together. "You were here, Olly. How could you, in any way whatsoever, believe that you are to blame?"

Millions of nervous trembles skittered over her skin. "I was so tired. We'd been putting in a lot of hours at the shop, and with all the Christmas shopping and wrapping and… God, it sounds so stupid now! But there was so much going on, and I'd totally forgotten to take Cody to see Santa earlier in the week." She wiped a stray tear from her cheek. Hell, she hadn't even realized she'd started to cry. "He was relentless in wanting to go, and we were running out of time. So…I told him to ask you. And when you came to me, I—"

"Suggested that Cody and I go alone, as a father-and-son outing."

"Yep. Because the idea of a few hours to myself seemed...heavenly." She lifted her gaze to meet her husband's. "When the police came here that night, I was in my bathrobe drinking a glass of wine and reading a book. I was *annoyed* when the doorbell rang, Grady. I wasn't in the mood for company. I—" She angrily wiped at the tears that refused to stop falling. "I remember thinking 'Great, I finally get some time to myself and someone has to show up and interrupt it.'"

She waited for Grady to say something—anything— but he didn't. He just stood there and looked at her with those dark, dark eyes of his. Her confession should have elicited some type of a response—a burst of anger, or a sigh of distress, or...

"Olivia," he said calmly, as if he were addressing a child, "you did not cause the accident. You are not at fault for the death of our son."

"Rationally, I know that. But I...am to blame for you and Cody going out that afternoon." She was surprised to hear how calm *she* sounded. "If I had remembered to take him when I was supposed to, you would have been home. If I had gone with you, as you wanted me to, then maybe...maybe—" Her breaths were coming too fast, too harsh. The walls were pushing in around her, suffocating her. "Maybe it would have been me instead of him. I was his mother. It was my job to protect him. But I chose to be alone."

"Olivia..."

"No, Grady, don't you see? I chose to be alone, and now he's gone, and guess what? I *am* alone!" Red-hot tears blinded her vision. "I *deserve* to be alone. It's what I wished for, after all."

"You didn't wish for our son's death!"

"No! But—" All at once, every pain she'd held on to

exploded through her body in a rush of raw awareness. Her sobs spilled from a place deep within, a place she had never allowed herself to poke at...to see what resided there. Now she knew. "It feels as if I did," she whispered brokenly. "I feel as if I brought this upon myself...upon us."

"Sweetheart, no." Grady came to her then. He pulled a chair up to hers and sat down, gripped her hands in his. "Listen to me, baby. You think I never had moments where I wanted an hour or two alone? Of course I did. Parenting is hard work. Life is busy. But you were there for Cody every single day. And you were an amazing mother."

"Then why is he gone?" she asked, staring steadfastly at the floor. "Why, Grady?"

"I don't know. But it isn't because of you or me. That is the one thing I know for sure."

She pulled one hand out of his grasp and fisted it against her chest. "It hurts. Right here. All of the time. And I don't know how to feel better."

"My therapist has this thing she says, 'Every person's path to healing is different. Some need to get there quicker, so they hop on the express lane.'" Grady's eyes softened. "'Others need to take the long, windy road and examine every stone along the way.'"

"I guess I'm examining stones, huh?"

"I guess so." Grady whisked his knuckles lightly across her cheek. "But the point is, you're heading in the right direction. So you go ahead and pick up every stone you want, sweetheart. Just promise me you'll keep moving forward."

"I am, Grady. I know that now. But you have to stop making decisions for me."

He acknowledged her statement with a short nod. "My

intentions have always been good. I've only wanted to help."

"I know, and you have in lots of ways." Tiredly, she shook her head. Everything that needed to be said jumbled together in her brain, leaving her numb. "I'm exhausted. I can't dig at this any more tonight."

"Right," he said, coughing to clear his throat. "I...I'll take off, then."

He returned his chair to its proper spot on the other side of the table before putting on his coat. She stood to walk him to the door. His leaving felt wrong, but she knew if she asked him to stay—even if only to sleep on the couch—he'd get the wrong impression. Well, hell, maybe it would be the right impression. She was too confused, too drained, at the moment to make any type of a serious decision. Heck, choosing which pajamas to wear to bed that night would likely prove to be a conundrum.

At the door, Grady said, "Tonight sucked. I'm sorry about that."

"It did suck," she agreed, still reeling from the emotional onslaught. "But you were right. We needed to have that conversation. I...I think in the long run, I'll feel better because of it."

"I feel the same." He brought his hand up, as if he were going to touch her cheek or stroke her hair, but must have thought better of it. "Give me a call or something, Olly. Whenever you're ready to talk about...well, whatever. Anything. I'll be around."

"Don't forget our fourth date," she said lightly, suddenly worried. "When is that, anyway? Next weekend?"

"No more dates. No more deal." He bent down and kissed the top of her head. "You know what I want. The rest is up to you."

"You can't do that. We had an agreement, Grady!"

A relieved grin surfaced. "So you want to keep going?"

"A deal is a deal, buddy." She squinted up at him. "As long as we're done with the bereavement group. If that's your plan, then I'm out."

A pained expression crossed his features. "Point taken. But no...I actually think you'll quite like what I have in mind for date number four." He shrugged. "Though, I've been known to be wrong before."

Standing up on her tiptoes, it was her turn to drop a light kiss on him. She chose his cheek. It felt scratchy and warm and oh-so-inviting. "So...next weekend?"

"Yeah," he said. "Next weekend."

"Okay. I'll see you then."

She locked the door behind him, but went to the living room to stand by the tree and look out the window. She watched as his headlights backed down her driveway and then sped away. Wishes and dreams and questions and worries tangled together in her mind, in her heart. She had a lot to figure out—about herself, about Grady and about their marriage.

But there was one thing she now knew for certain: the ice queen was gone forever. And thank God for that.

Chapter Ten

Thursday afternoon found Grady in a seriously bad mood. Olivia hadn't returned any of his phone calls that week, let alone actually answered any of the times he'd tried to reach her. Initially, he'd been worried. Worried enough that he'd driven to the house last night to check on her, only to discover she wasn't home. And because he'd given his key back, he couldn't even let himself in to ascertain that everything was as it should be.

Finally, he phoned Sammy. Who'd laughingly assured him that Olivia was fine. She'd also pointed out that giving Olly some time to sort through everything wouldn't be a bad idea. And it wasn't. But that didn't brighten his mood any.

His wife's confession had shocked him to the very core. His heart ached for what she'd gone through, for the torment she'd lived with. But now, so much of her past behavior made sense. He got it. Finally. He'd left her house

Saturday night feeling optimistic. Mostly because she'd insisted on keeping their agreement in force when he was prepared to let it go.

She *wanted* the fourth date.

Unfortunately, his optimism had long since faded to pessimism. He'd given a lot of thought to how *he'd* behaved, and he was ashamed to see himself through Olivia's eyes. He *had* tried to make decisions for her. Sure, his reasoning was solid: he wanted to help her. But how often had he actually shut up and listened to her? Not often enough.

So that, combined with her recent avoidance, which felt too familiar for his comfort, had set his mind on the possibility that she was rearing up to go through with the divorce. He still didn't want it. He still believed that they could be happy again. In truth, he believed this more now than he had for years. The last several weeks had proven to him that Olivia was ready to live again. That was the good news.

But damn, he wanted to be a part of that life.

"You're looking awfully dour," Jace said, strolling into the back office at Foster's Auto Concepts. "Contemplating the fate of humankind?"

Grady shook off his musings and tried for a realistic-sounding laugh. "Nah. Scouring the internet for the perfect Christmas gift for you. Can't decide between the books *Relationships for Dummies* or *Romance for Dummies.*" Giving Jace a look of mock seriousness, he said, "Which do you think will prove more beneficial to your recent woman problems?"

Jace scowled and dropped into one of the chairs. "Bite me."

"No, thanks." Giving up the joke, Grady said, "What brings you here on a Thursday afternoon unannounced?"

"Olivia," Jace replied. "She called me this morning."

"For?"

"She wanted to know where Seth and I stored the presents you guys bought for Cody before…umm…you know." Jace shifted in discomfort. "She said they used to be in the garage? But she can't find them now. And…dude… Seth and I didn't touch those gifts. We only dealt with the decorations."

"I moved them to the attic," Grady said, trying to figure out what Olivia wanted with Cody's presents. "I wanted to donate them to charity but didn't feel I should without her okay. Did she say why she was looking for them?"

"Nope." Jace picked up a pencil from Grady's desk. "But she seemed flustered when I told her we hadn't touched them. I'm surprised she hasn't contacted you about it."

"Me, too." Grady narrowed his eyes at his brother, sensing there was something else up. "You could've called me with this information. Why the personal visit?"

"No reason in particular." Jace tapped the pencil against the surface of the desk and averted his gaze. "Why the third degree? Can't I stop in to see my brother?"

Ah. This was about the woman in Jace's office. "Look. I'm sorry I teased you about the *Dummies* books. If there's something you want to ask me, ask. That's…uh…what big brothers are for." Not that Grady was all that great at offering advice about women, but he'd give it a shot.

"I want to give her a Christmas gift," Jace said hurriedly, still not looking at Grady. "But I don't know if I should. Or if she'll even accept it if I do. But I want to. I found out kind of accidentally, kind of on purpose, that she collects antique dolls."

"Uh-huh," Grady said. "I'm not going to ask how you managed to gather information in an accidentally, on-purpose sort of way, but go on."

Deep red circles appeared on Jace's cheeks. "Don't be an ass. This is hard for me."

"Sorry."

"So...umm...I was shopping over the weekend for the family, right? And I came across this antique store, and I don't know much about dolls, but there was one... I don't know, she reminded me of Melanie. I know she'd love it."

A name, finally. Grady kept his jaw firmly shut, and nodded.

"I bought it. The doll. But now I don't know how to give this to Melanie...or, you know, if I even should. Or if she'll accept it."

"You mentioned that." Grady worked to stay straight-faced. Not all that easy, but he pulled it off. "Women tend to like receiving gifts. And at Christmas, I'm not sure how you can go wrong."

"This is dumb, right? Being so worked-up about giving a woman a Christmas present?"

"I wouldn't say dumb," Grady said carefully. "Perhaps you should consider why you're so worked up?"

"Because I want her to have this. I know she'll love the doll. But she—" Jace coughed. "She has this impression of me."

"Playboy," Grady interjected. "So? You're working on changing that. Giving her a gift you know she'll enjoy might help her see you in a different light."

Jace's scowl deepened. "Nope. She'll think I'm using the doll to get in her pants."

"Are you?"

"No. And I don't want her to think that."

"Then give it to her anonymously," Grady suggested. "Sign the card 'Your Secret Santa' or something. She'll probably love that." Olivia used to love the surprise gifts and cards he'd leave her here and there. Hmm. He hadn't done that in a while.

Jace's expression lightened immediately. "That's a great idea. And maybe someday, the situation will be different and I can tell her the doll came from me."

"Okay, then. There you go. Problem solved." Damn. Once again, Grady was jealous of Jace. If only his women problems had such an easy fix. Maybe he was the one who needed the *Dummies* book. "Glad to be of service."

Olivia tugged at her sweater, wishing it didn't hang on her frame so loosely. Not that it mattered. She could poke two holes in a garbage bag to stick her arms through and prance around in that and Grady wouldn't notice. But for today—their fourth date—she wanted to look beautiful. More important, she wanted to *feel* beautiful.

She sprayed some perfume on her wrists and behind her ears, and then applied a coat of lip gloss. Stepping back, she took in her full appearance. "Not too bad," she whispered. "Even with the baggy sweater."

Her legs looked long and lean in her skinny jeans, and her hair was lustrous and shiny. That, she knew, was because of the ultrapricey shampoo and conditioner she'd bought the last time she'd had her hair styled. She'd gone light on cosmetics, but even so, her eyes appeared bluer than normal and her cheeks held a healthy glow.

Yep. She was ready. Glancing at the clock, she saw the time: eight o'clock. Grady would be arriving any minute. Where they were going so early on a Saturday morning, she didn't have a clue. And he, when she'd phoned him last night, hadn't shared their destination.

But she was excited. Anticipation for the day ahead brought a sheath of goose bumps to her arms and a bounce to her step. Today, her goal was to have fun. With Grady.

Hopefully, his mind-set was the same. She wasn't even to the bottom of the stairs when the bell rang.

She opened the door and grinned. "Hey, you. Where are we off to so early?"

"Hey, you, back." Grady's eyes widened in appreciation. Score one for her. "Wow, Olly. You look gorgeous. Happy."

Feeling saucy, she winked. "You look pretty good yourself." And, oh, God, did he ever. His chocolate-brown V-neck sweater was worn over a white T-shirt, and his boot-cut jeans fit in such a way that they showed off his narrow hips and muscular thighs.

A ruddy flush stole over Grady's cheeks. Jeez, how long had it been since she'd given him a compliment? "Grab your coat and we'll get going. We have a drive ahead of us."

"Oh, yeah? Where to?" she asked, getting her coat from the closet.

"Bend," he said, holding her coat while she slid her arms into the sleeves. "I thought we could check out the Old Mill District. Maybe do some shopping, if you're not done already. You know," he said softly, "do the Christmas thing."

Going to Bend, Oregon, during the holiday season was something she and Grady had done every year before Cody was born. After... Well, there never seemed to be enough time. And a nearly three-hour car ride with a child who could hardly stand to sit still seemed silly. But for today? She couldn't have come up with a better plan herself.

"Oh! What a wonderful idea," she said, sure she was glowing on the outside as well as on the inside. "And I do have some shopping left to take care of."

"Before we leave, did you need some help in getting those presents down from the attic?"

When they spoke the previous night, Grady had told her where Cody's presents were. She'd been surprised when he brought the topic up, but she should have realized that Jace would mention her call. Grady didn't ask what her motivation was in finding them, and she didn't share. There would be plenty of time for that…if she followed through. "I…umm…haven't decided on that yet. If I do, I'll let you know."

Curiosity colored his gaze, but he didn't question her further. "Well, then. Let's get moving. I thought if we got there by eleven, we could grab some lunch before the noon rush."

"Mmm. Do you know if they have snow?" She followed him out and down the driveway, to where his pickup was parked. She had this image of them walking through softly falling snow, hand in hand, with snowflakes melting on their cheeks.

"Baby, it's Bend in December. What do you think?"

This, she realized with a start, was the first time in forever that she'd thought of snow as anything other than an enemy. Another shot of warmth suffused her. "Good," she said, opening the passenger door to Grady's truck. There, resting on the seat, was a silver-wrapped box with a bright red bow stuck on top. She carefully picked up the present and hopped in the truck. When Grady slid into the driver's seat, she asked, "What is this?"

His eyes rounded in mock surprise. "Where did you get that?"

"On my seat. Where you left it."

"Hmm. Wasn't me, Olly. And it wasn't there before," he said, firing up the ignition.

"Sure it wasn't," she said, trying hard not to laugh.

"So…maybe someone has a crush on you, Grady? This being your truck and all."

"Ah…maybe. Why don't you see if there's a card attached?" Damn, he was good. His voice held all the right notes. "But I'm telling you, I have no idea where that came from."

"You forget how well *I* know *you*," she said with a grin. And yeah, her bones were doing that melting thing again. "How many cards and flowers and other presents have you secretly given me over the years, hmm?"

"I don't believe we ever ascertained who your secret admirer was." Grady pulled onto the street and tossed her a sidelong glance. "Maybe he's back. Maybe his life got crazy and he forgot to remind you of how special you are to him. Maybe this is his way of saying he's sorry."

Fizzy bubbles of warmth and pleasure widened her smile. But she didn't move to open the present. She couldn't. Not when her attention was so wholly captured by the man sitting next to her. "You're an incredible man, Grady Foster," she said softly.

The ruddy flush returned. "You check that card yet?"

"No, but I will now." She peeled off the tiny envelope taped to the silver wrapping. Using the tip of her nail, she slit open the envelope. The card inside featured a round, chubby puppy with floppy ears and a pair of fake reindeer antlers stuck to his head. She opened the card and read, "Each day brings us the opportunity to create new memories. Here's hoping you'll remember this day with joy."

"Well, whomever your admirer is, he sure isn't a poet," Grady said with a little cough. "But I suppose the sentiment is nice."

"No, Grady. The sentiment is wonderful." She turned

the present over in her hands, feeling like a very lucky woman. "Should I open this now or wait for Christmas?"

"I would think he'd want you to open it now."

"Right. Whoever this mysterious 'he' is." She carefully removed the wrapping to find a white square box. She lifted the lid. Inside was an ornament no larger than the size of her palm. But it was gorgeous. A 3-D crystal snowflake that sparkled as if it were made of diamonds. The weight of the ornament was heavy and solid, and she knew that when hung on the tree, the lights would make it glitter all that much more. "This is beautiful, Grady. Thank you."

This time, he didn't try to pretend the gift wasn't from him. "I thought you might want a new ornament for the tree. Something to—" he shrugged as he turned onto the expressway "—begin a memory for this Christmas."

She held the snowflake up to the window. The sun shone in and through the ornament, turning the snowflake into a prism. Suddenly, a rainbow of colors filled the interior of the truck. "And yes, Grady," she said, awestruck by the display of colors bouncing and bobbing around her. "I will definitely remember this moment...this day...with joy."

After tucking the ornament safely into its box, she leaned against the seat cushion. She was very much looking forward to the rest of what today had to offer. Grady turned on the radio and Christmas music poured from the speakers.

"So, tell me more about this girl Jace is interested in," she said. "You think he's serious?"

Warm laughter tumbled from Grady's mouth. "Yeah, he's serious. He bought her a gift...."

Grady continued to talk. Not only about Jace, but about work, his family and a host of other topics as he drove.

Every now and then, she'd add her share to the conversation, but mostly, she settled in and enjoyed the sound of her husband's voice.

Several hours later, they were strolling in and out of shops in the Old Mill District of Bend. They'd gotten into the city slightly after eleven, and by the time they found a restaurant, she'd been half nauseous, half starving. Not that odd, seeing how she'd skipped breakfast, but she'd worried she might be catching the flu that was going around at work.

Luckily, a bowl of chicken noodle soup and her half of the sandwich she and Grady had split fixed her right up. Now, they were attempting to get some Christmas shopping done. She'd already bought two small gifts for Samantha, as well as a couple of new ornaments to hang on her tree at home. She noticed that Grady had chosen a few toys here and there. Toys that were appropriate for eight-year-old boys, but she didn't call him out on it. After all, if she wanted him to respect her needs, then she had to respect his.

She'd almost purchased such a toy herself. A rather awesome art kit that came with everything a child's imagination could possibly want: crayons, colored pencils, paper of various sizes, modeling clay, craft glue, pipe cleaners and so much more. In the end, though, she decided not to. For one, the kit was rather large and cumbersome, and she didn't relish the thought of carrying it around all day. Nor did she want Grady to. For two, she wasn't quite ready. Maybe next year.

"Look at that," Grady said, as they stepped out of a quaint shop filled to the brim with everything and anything related to Christmas. He pointed to a horse-drawn sleigh that was making its way down the street. "Feel like taking a ride?"

"I would love to," she said. "Do you think we can?"

"I don't see why not. We just have to figure out where to go." Grady glanced up one side of the street and down the other. "Wait here, and I'll run back in to ask the shop clerk."

While waiting, she gawked at the dazzling displays that almost every store on the street had. Obviously, there were Christmas lights everywhere. But there were also a variety of holiday animatronics that made children and adults stop and stare in awe. If was almost as if she'd stepped into a snow globe of the perfect Christmas village.

Well, without the snow. Oh, there was plenty of the white stuff on the ground, but there wasn't a real snowflake to be seen. She tipped her head toward the beauty of Mt. Hood. Up there, she was sure, were plenty of snowflakes whistling through the air.

Grady returned with the news that sleigh rides were available from another store down the road from where they currently stood. They took their time getting there, stopping in a few other shops on their way. After all, the day was still early and there was nothing neither of them had to do that night.

Well, Olivia admitted to herself, there was something she'd like to do that night. She was almost there...almost ready to tell Grady everything that was in her heart.

But she had to be sure. She refused to give him false hope until she was.

Grady folded Olivia's smaller hand in his and settled in for the sleigh ride he'd promised her. He hoped she wouldn't be disappointed. "The driver was telling me about this place fifteen miles outside of the city," he said. "Sunriver Resort. Apparently, they have holiday events happening every weekend."

"A resort? I've never heard of it."

"Me, either. But it's supposed to be really special. Maybe something to keep in mind for next—" He coughed to cover the word *year*. He had no idea where they'd be in a year. "Next time you come out this way," he said, completing his sentence.

"That sounds nice. But I'm having a great time right here, right now."

If he'd known about Sunriver Resort, they'd have gone there today. And, instead of a quick sleigh ride through the streets he and Olly had already walked, Sunriver's sleigh rides were supposedly an experience not to be missed. Cozy blankets, hot chocolate and that whole dashing-through-the-snow thing. With bells actually jingling, even. Ah, well. He couldn't have planned what he hadn't known about.

"Are you?" he asked in all seriousness. "You've been a little quiet."

"Just soaking in the atmosphere. I truly am enjoying myself, Grady," she promised, squeezing his hand. "Everything feels magical, doesn't it?"

He nodded, not able to talk.

"The only thing missing is snow." She looked up at him with sparkling blue eyes and pink-from-the-cold cheeks. "I wanted to catch snowflakes on my tongue," she admitted sheepishly. "Silly, huh?"

"Maybe a little," he agreed. "But also endearing."

One of the horses whinnied as they rounded the corner of the street they were on. The carriage driver pointed out a few of the shops as they traveled and gave a rundown of some of the events happening around the city. Olivia leaned forward to ask a few questions.

Grady was grateful, as his thoughts were elsewhere. Olivia hadn't mentioned anything about their marriage or the divorce or her thoughts on either. When he'd questioned her about not returning his phone calls, she'd claimed a busy week as her excuse, and yeah, that was probably true. Realistically, though, it only takes a minute to phone someone. So he had to wonder what was going on inside of her head.

Olivia sighed. "This is so lovely. I hate for the day to end."

And with those seven little words, some of Grady's worry dissipated. "We have hours before we have to head home. Once we're done shopping, I thought we could do a little ice-skating. Maybe see if we can find some caroling later, and then grab dinner before going home."

"Wow, you really thought this out."

"They're only ideas, Olly." He formed the cross sign over his heart with his fingers. "Boy Scout's honor. If there's an activity you have in mind, say the word. I'm up for anything. Or—" he shrugged "—we can go home early."

"I've never ice-skated. Only in-line skated. And even then, I wasn't all that graceful. But why not? What's the worst that can happen?" She screwed her nose up. "Other than breaking my ankle or leg or arm, that is."

"If you start to fall, I'll throw my body in front of yours to protect you." He slid a stray strand of hair behind her ear, relishing the ability touch her. "You can fall on me."

"Such a gentleman." The words were said with a teasing lilt, but unasked questions gleamed in her eyes. He'd noticed the same silent, assessing regard earlier, over lunch. It killed him not to ask her what she was thinking. "So, ice-skating, huh? I'm assuming they rent out skates?" she asked.

"Let's hope so. Otherwise, we'll have to glide around the pond in our shoes," he replied, trying to replicate her lighthearted tone. "And all the other skaters will laugh and point at us."

She did that nose-wrinkle thing again, and it was all he could do not to lean over and kiss her. Damn, he wanted to kiss her.

"Skates or no, I definitely want to check it out." She poked him in his side. "Even if we're ridiculed for coming unprepared."

Over his shoulder, the carriage driver announced that they were on the last block of their ride. A small, disappointed sigh floated from Olivia to Grady. In that second, he promised himself that even if he couldn't take her to Sunriver Resort next year, he'd make sure she went. Maybe with Samantha. Or maybe with another man. The thought sent a stiff shudder of jealousy through Grady, but he couldn't deny that the possibility existed.

And, jealousy or no, he wanted her to be happy above all else. So if their relationship ended and a new man was able to give her what he couldn't…he'd wish her well. And then, he'd have to learn how to live without her.

Chapter Eleven

Wind filled with the promise of snow blustered and blew around Olivia as she attempted to put on her ice skates. Grady had found a man-made pond on the outskirts of Bend. The entire area was decked out in holiday charm, and made Olivia think she had stepped into a Christmas movie. There were white lights strung through trees, holiday music blaring from speakers that surrounded the pond, hot chocolate and roasted chestnuts being sold, and smiling people everywhere she looked. And, yes, the establishment rented out ice skates.

Grady knelt in front of her to make sure her skates' laces were securely tied. Standing, he held out his hand. "Ready to give this a try?" he asked.

"You grew up on these things. Please remember that I didn't."

"I told you, you have nothing to fear." He lightly tugged, helping her to stand. "I won't let you fall, sweetheart."

Slowly, they made their way to the ice. There, Grady faced her and held both of her hands. Then, as people who seemingly were born with a pair of ice skates on their feet raced past them, Grady skated backward at a leisurely pace, pulling her along with him.

She felt as awkward as a newborn colt appears, but she kept her gaze plastered to Grady's, focused on her balance and somehow managed to stay upright.

"You're doing wonderfully, Olly," Grady said encouragingly. "You're a natural."

"I'm not sure about that, but this is fun." And it was. Her body soon found the proper rhythm and before too long, she felt comfortable enough to continue talking. "I've always wanted to learn how to ice-skate," she confided. "When I was little, I told my mom I wanted to be a figure skater when I grew up."

"Really? You never shared that with me," Grady said, increasing their speed from a snail's pace to that of a lumbering tortoise. "What did good ole' Jilly have to say about that?"

In the ten years that they'd been together, Grady had only met her parents twice. It was during their first meeting that he'd started calling Olivia's slightly standoffish and oh-so-proper mother "Jilly." A nickname that Olivia's father had found all too humorous. Her mother, on the other hand, hated it. Which wasn't a surprise. She hated being called Mom, too.

Olivia grinned. "*Jillian* said that to be good at figure skating, one has to spend countless amounts of hours and money on lessons, and she didn't have the money and I didn't have the patience." Olivia shrugged and almost lost her balance. Once she recovered, she said, "Can't say she was wrong on either account."

"That doesn't sound like you." Grady slowed them

down again as they came around the curve on the far side of the pond. "I've always known you to be patient."

"In some things. But when I was a kid, if I wasn't good at something right off the bat, I'd get frustrated and give up."

Grady nodded. "Oh, I see. That perfectionist thing. Yep, I definitely get that."

She narrowed her eyes. "You're one to talk. I used to call you Mr. Fix-it." A tiny grin lifted the corners of her lips. "Sometimes I still do."

"Well, I used to call you…" His voice trailed off. Glints of humor lit up his eyes. "Never mind. I have nothing."

"Your attempt at a sarcastic comeback is duly noted. As is your failure in finding one," she teased. "You'll think of something tomorrow, I'm sure."

"I'm sure," he responded dryly. "So, do you think you're ready to try this side by side?"

"Umm…I don't know. Why don't we go all the way around one more time, and then we'll give the arm-in-arm thing a shot?" She'd be fine now. But she loved the intimacy of looking her husband in the eyes as they skated.

As if he'd read her mind, a silent but potent sizzle of electricity passed between them and her knees felt like melted butter. She stumbled, sure she was about to get up close and personal with the ice, when Grady's arms pulled her straight to him. She heard the swish of his skates grabbing on to the ice, his legs locked, and she halted against his chest midfall.

"Gotcha," he whispered, his lips near her ear. "Told you I wouldn't let you fall, baby."

And then, magic happened. She lifted her chin to look into his eyes, and a big, fat, icy snowflake landed on her forehead, another on her cheek. And when she opened her mouth…she caught a couple on her tongue. "It's snow-ing! Look, Grady!"

"I can't," he said, sounding strangely muffled. "Not when you're so beautiful my eyes don't see anything else."

"Oh," she whispered. Her heart fluttered in her chest, like a million and one butterfly wings. This time, though, she didn't feel as if they were trying to escape. With great care, she caressed his cheek with her hand, and the ques-tion in her mind tumbled off her tongue effortlessly. "Will you kiss me, Grady?"

"I thought you'd never ask." The deep, husky rumble of his voice held nuances of need…want…desire. And yes, love. So much love that she trembled.

Another snowflake dropped to her nose as their lips met. His kiss…*this* kiss…was tender and sweet, fiery and intense. And oh-so-intimate. She forgot they were stand-ing outside, on a frozen pond, with who knew how many people around them. She forgot she wore ice skates. She… Well, she forgot everything.

His mouth firmed on hers. He tasted of the cinnamon-laced hot chocolate and spicy roasted chestnuts they'd consumed when first arriving at the pond. His tongue prodded her lips open and slipped inside, and tiny, barely heard gurgles of pleasure tickled her throat.

Oh, God. She loved this man so very much. And oh, how she wanted him. In her bed, in her life, in every min-ute of every day, in every way possible, she wanted Grady.

The kiss came to an end and they pulled apart care-fully. Grady kept his arms tight around her so she wouldn't fall. He grinned in that lopsided way that reminded her so much of Cody.

"I love…" He paused. "I love this day, Olly. But we should probably head home. We have a long drive and the snow," he said as he looked up, "seems to be coming down harder."

She swallowed. She *knew* he loved her. She *knew* that was what he'd almost said. Why hadn't he? "Good idea," she whispered. "But sad, too. It probably isn't snowing in Portland."

"Probably not." Together, they skated off of the ice. As soon as they'd turned in their ice skates and recovered their shoes, they walked toward the truck. "Are you hungry? We can stop and get some dinner once we're out of the snow."

"Why don't we wait until we get to the house? My stomach is filled with cocoa and chestnuts, so I'm good for a while." Besides, as silly as it might sound, she felt like she needed an excuse to invite Grady in. "I can make us dinner."

Once the truck was warmed up, Olivia removed her coat and stuck it behind her head as a pillow. She yawned and closed her eyes, exhausted from the outdoor activity. And, when Grady covered her with his coat, she pulled it around her and savored his scent. The hum of the engine combined with her tiredness put her to sleep almost immediately.

She woke with a start when Grady's arm slammed into her. She shot straight up in her seat, her heart pounding in what felt like a million beats per second. Grady cursed as he maneuvered the truck with one hand, keeping his other arm protectively on Olivia. She instantly saw what was happening. There was an accident ahead of them, and one car after another was sliding into the accident, unable to stop quickly enough on the snow- and ice-slicked road.

"My seat belt is on, Grady," she said in a fear-choked voice. "Use both hands on the wheel."

He complied but kept his attention on trying to keep

them out of danger. She watched in horror as the vehicle three up from theirs slammed into another car. Grady cussed again, and said, "Hold on, sweetheart. I'm taking us off the road."

He turned the steering wheel hard to the right. They literally missed hitting the car in front of them by seconds. Olivia couldn't breathe as Grady guided the truck toward the only spot she saw vacant of trees. What appeared to be a very, very narrow spot. She closed her eyes and prayed the truck would stop moving. Prayed they wouldn't hit anything. Prayed for their safety. She felt the tires slide and she squeezed her hands into tight fists. The truck bumped and groaned over uneven snow-covered ground and the sound seemed to be excruciatingly loud.

Her head slammed back against the seat cushion when they came to an abrupt stop. Tremors whipped through her body, shaking her muscles and her bones, clattering her teeth. She tried to breathe to calm herself, tried to bring herself down from the mountain of panicked fear she stood upon. This...

"Open your eyes, Olly," Grady's tense voice reached her ears. "We're okay. I'm okay. So are you, honey."

"Those people," she murmured. "We need to get help." The words were barely out of her mouth when she heard sirens. Okay, help was already here. "How bad is it, Grady?" she asked, afraid to open her eyes to look.

"Bad," he said grimly. "There are at least half a dozen cars clumped together up there. Come on. We need to see what's going on. If there's anything we can do to help. And we'll need to get a tow truck out here."

"Yes, of course." She snapped her eyes open. She had to focus on what needed to be done. Later, she could think about what had almost happened. Again.

Tragedy. It seemed to be right around the corner, lurking, always waiting to strike. And this time, it could have stolen Grady from her. She'd come so close to losing someone else she loved.

Grady came around to her side of the truck to help her out. She handed him his coat and put her coat on. They were lucky. Very, very lucky. Not only had Grady managed to avoid the accident, but he'd gotten the truck stopped without colliding into any of the massive trees littering this section of the landscape. Yes. Luck. But could she count on luck being there the next time tragedy decided to visit?

In slow, sluggish steps, they made their way to the accident site. People were everywhere. Some were crying, others were rushing around in their need to help, and some were being tended to by the paramedics. She counted four ambulances in all, two of which sped off with patients needing immediate care.

Sickness lurched in her stomach. She ordered herself to pull it together. Grady led her to a police officer, and they gave their statement of what occurred...of what they saw. It was almost two hours later before the truck was towed back onto the road, and another hour before they were able to once again head for home.

Olivia didn't sleep this time, nor did she talk. Grady didn't, either. His body was tense and stiff the entire way to her house, and his eyes never left the road. When they pulled into her driveway, she turned toward him.

"I know I talked about making dinner, but I just want to crawl in bed and sleep. And... Well, I need some time to think about everything." She shook her head, feeling numb and empty and scared. So very scared. "I'm shaken, I guess. Too much right now to...to..."

"I'm shaken too, Olly." His voice whispered over her, and she heard his fear as clear as day. And, as scared as she was, it had to have been worse for him. It had to have reminded him of the night their son died. "I... God. It makes a man never want to drive again."

"I know."

"I'm glad you're okay." His voice thickened and caught. "So damn glad."

"I'm glad you're okay, too," she said brokenly. For once, though, there were no tears in her eyes. They'd been wrung out of her, she guessed. "When...when is the six weeks up?" she said, hating herself the second the words spilled from her mouth. The real question, the one she'd meant to ask, burned in her brain. *How long will you wait for me, Grady? How long until you give up on me?* "When...when do I need to have this figured out by?"

Agony pierced his expression. Also, a fair amount of frustration. She couldn't blame him for that. "December 26, Olly. The day after Christmas. So almost two weeks. But take all the time you need." Then, he looked away from her. "I'll let you know if I...get tired of waiting."

Right. Well, she couldn't expect him to wait forever, now could she?

The next day, Olivia arrived at Samantha's with two bottles of wine, her pajamas, and the entire *Die Hard* collection of movies. Young or not so young, she adored Bruce Willis. And Sam freaking panted whenever he came on-screen. Her friend answered the door on the second knock, and Olivia grinned. Sam had obviously already started her homemade spaghetti sauce. The proof was written all over her white and reddish-orange splashed T-shirt.

"Come in and—" Samantha's gaze fell on the bag Olivia held. "Do you have wine?"

"I do."

"You, my dear, are a saint. I meant to buy some when I hit the grocery store this morning, but spaced out." Samantha took one of the bags from Olivia's hands. "Come in. I've been looking forward to this all week. Any problems taking tomorrow off?"

"Nope. I think they were relieved I was finally using some of my personal time." She slid by Samantha to enter the apartment. "I actually ended up taking the entire week off, and we're always closed the week of Christmas. So I'm footloose and fancy-free." Hey, it sounded good, even if she didn't actually feel all that fancy-free. "What about you? Are you going in tomorrow or hanging with me?"

"Haven't decided yet. I'll definitely go in late, though." They went to the kitchen, where Samantha immediately opened one of the bottles of wine. "Want a glass?"

"Maybe later. But I could use a soda." Olivia had barely slept the night before, what with the images of the accident replaying themselves over and over behind her closed eyelids. To make everything even worse, she'd woken up that morning with a slightly off stomach. Brought on by nerves, she figured. "Ginger ale if you have it."

Samantha rolled her eyes. "I'm not your maid. Help yourself."

Olivia found a lone can of ginger ale amidst an ocean of colas. Taking it, she sat on one of the bar stools and watched Samantha doctor the bubbling pot of sauce with a variety of spices. Faint nausea climbed her throat. She combated it by sipping her soda.

And, because she needed to talk about it, she launched into the story of what went down with Grady yesterday. She didn't skip over anything. Bit by bit, she led Samantha through the day—from the moment Grady had picked her up until the second he brought her home, and every detail in between.

"Holy crap, Olivia. You could've died." Samantha turned the heat down on the sauce. "Or Grady. Or both of you."

"I know." She'd listened to the news this morning, and was relieved to hear that while there had been injuries, no one had lost their life. "It was scary, Sam."

Visibly rattled, Sam went to Olivia and gave her a quick hug. "I can only imagine. Grady must have been out of his mind. What with—" She chomped down on her lip and shook her head. "Sorry."

"It's okay," Olivia said, knowing she'd trained Samantha to not bring up any mention of Cody. "You can say it. No more treating me with kid gloves. Okay?"

Samantha blinked several times. Probably in surprise. "Okay. It might take me a while to get used to that, but good for you, Olivia. Really. What I was going to say was that going through another accident must have taken Grady back to the accident with Cody. That had to have freaked him out."

"I think it did. But he…he kept his cool until we were safe. I don't know how he managed that." The more Olivia thought about last night, the more impressed she was with how Grady had handled the crisis. Tough, strong and in control. "I was a basket case."

"Of course you were. I would've been, too."

"I doubt that. You're always so…contained and capable."

Samantha did sort of a snort-giggle. "You don't know me as well as you think you do. Though, I agree with the capable assessment." She paused. "So, any chance you feel like discussing the hours *before* the accident?"

"I told you everything, already. It was wonderful. Enchanting. The perfect day." God. The smell of the spaghetti sauce was really doing a number on her stomach.

She drank some more ginger ale. "Is there anything specific you want to know?"

"Do you know what you're going to do?"

"No. Yes. Hell, I don't know. I change my mind every five minutes." Grady's parting statement sifted into her consciousness. "But I think Grady's tired of waiting. He...ah...told me to take all the time I needed, but that he'd let me know if...well, if he got tired of waiting."

Samantha scooted onto the stool next to Olivia. "Hey, this is fun." At Olivia's questioning glance, she continued, "Having you actually answer my questions instead of changing the topic or giving me a half-baked reply."

"About that, Sam." Inhaling a deep, fortifying breath, Olivia said, "I realized that I haven't been the friend to you that you've been to me. I'm sorry. Really sorry. But I am so grateful you've stuck around." Olivia smiled to show her sincerity. "And I can't promise that being open and forthcoming will stick, but I'm trying."

"Aw, Olivia...you've totally been worth waiting for." Leaning forward, Samantha rested her chin on her laced-together fingers. Giving Olivia an intense look, she said, "Moving on...what's holding you back with Grady? I mean...you love him, he loves you, blah-blah-freaking-blah and happily-ever-after, right? What's the holdup, girl?"

With a totally straight face, Olivia said, "Jeez, Sam. I can't for the life of me figure out why you don't have a boyfriend."

"Hey. Don't you do that answer-a-question-with-a-sarcastic-statement thing. That's my thing!" Samantha flipped her hair over her shoulder. "And this conversation is about you."

"Fine. It's exactly what you said. The happily-ever-after thing."

"Should I understand the deeper meaning in that response?"

Olivia downed another mouthful of ginger ale. "I had the fairy tale once already. I believed in happily-ever-after once already. And look how that ended? I don't know if I can...*want* to go for it again. In some ways, life is easier *knowing* you can't have it all, even if that's because it's your choice." She shrugged, trying to appear nonchalant when, in fact, this dilemma was tearing her up inside. "And don't bother telling me that life is about the good and the bad and that we have to live every day to its fullest. I am rational enough to understand that argument. But guess what, Sam? Sometimes the heart isn't rational at all."

"Whoa girl, take a breath."

"A little overkill on the emotion, huh?"

Samantha squeezed two fingers together. "A tiny bit, yeah. Look...you're a smart woman. You're already going through all of this in your head, and only you know what you're capable of living with. And as much as I want to see you and Grady together again, I'm not you."

"If you were me, what would you do?"

"I haven't faced a tragedy like you have, my dear, so I can't really answer that. I think I would go for the brass ring again. I hope I would. Life is short, you know? But I can't be certain, and I'm not going to lie to you and say I can be."

"I appreciate your honesty. A ton. Thanks, Sam."

"That's what friends are for, right?"

"Absolutely. And if I want to talk just for the sake of hearing my own voice, you'll be happy to listen and nod your head, right?"

"I'm an attorney. I'm damn good at that." Sam laughed and nodded toward the pot of spaghetti sauce. "Now, I want that to simmer for a while. Want to keep chatting or go start a movie?"

"Movie, please." Hopefully, a few hours of a sexy man kicking ass and taking names would give her brain a much needed rest.

"Cool. I have a selection of classic Steven Segal ready and waiting. What did you bring?"

"Every *Die Hard* movie ever made." Olivia grinned at Samantha's grin. "Yep. I'm thinking Bruce, too."

Samantha grabbed the sofa before Olivia had the disc in the player, so Olivia mounded up some pillows and stretched out on the floor. The opening credits played, and then there he was: Bruce in all his glory.

Sam sighed from behind Olivia. "I need a Bruce," she said. "Where can I find one?"

"I don't know," Olivia answered in faux sympathy. "Perhaps you should ask Santa."

A throw pillow hit Olivia square on the head. "No more talking," Sam said. "Especially if you don't have any better advice than that!"

They watched the entire movie and half of another before Sam declared the spaghetti sauce was ready to be served. Back in the kitchen, Olivia tended to the cheesy-garlic bread sticks while Samantha simultaneously boiled pasta and made a salad. Within thirty minutes, they'd returned to the living room, started the movie where they left off, and dug in to dinner.

The first bite of spaghetti went down okay. The second, not so much. By the third, Olivia was racing to the bathroom with her hand over her mouth. She sat on the edge of the bathtub and willed her stomach to behave. When she felt rather sure her food would stay put, she washed her face with cold water and rejoined Samantha.

"Are you okay?" Sam asked.

"I don't know. Maybe I have the flu? I've been feeling off for a couple of days now. But there isn't any way I can eat, and that sucks. I love your spaghetti sauce." Olivia picked up her dinner plates and took them into the kitchen. Samantha followed. "I'm sorry. Maybe I should go home," Olivia said. "I don't want you to get sick."

"You know," Sam said carefully, with an odd look on her face. "I remember when you were pregnant with Cody, you couldn't even handle the smell of anything cooked with tomatoes. Is there something you *haven't* told me, Olivia?"

"What are you saying?" But then, the night Olivia spent with Grady clicked in her head. She quickly added up the dates. Oh, wow. "Umm…" She crossed to one of the stools and sat down before her legs gave out on her. And added up the dates again.

"Olivia?"

"Maybe," she said in a faint voice. "It's possible."

"Grady?"

"No," Olivia said flippantly. "A guy I met at the grocery store one night. Don't even know his name." She paused for dramatic effect. "Yes, Grady! Who else?"

"Well, crap, Olivia. You didn't tell me…not that you had to." Samantha sat next to Olivia. "When?"

"Umm…just about four weeks ago." Almost to the day. Plus two days, actually. "Four weeks and two days ago." *A baby?* Now? Try as she might, Olivia could not wrap her mind around this…but her heart was already expanding and softening and wishing.

"I take it you guys didn't use birth control?" Samantha asked, not bothering to hide the hint of humor in her voice. "You do know about birth control, right?"

Olivia swallowed. Hard. "It was spur-of-the-moment.

Neither of us planned it, Sam. And I certainly didn't think… Hadn't even considered…"

"Well, then your mama never taught you about the birds and the bees. It's like this, Olivia…a boy meets a girl, and sometimes, when the feelings are very, very strong—"

"It's probably just the flu. A stomach virus has been going around at work. So…this is probably nothing. A false alarm." Olivia closed her eyes and mentally envisioned a calendar, and added up the dates again. She had to be wrong.

But what if…what if she wasn't? Her hand found her stomach and a slow fizz of hope trickled through her. "Umm…Sam?"

"Want me to run to the drug store?"

God, she loved Samantha. "Yes, please. I think I'm just going to sit here."

"Move to the living room where the smell of the spaghetti isn't so strong." Samantha gently shoved her off the bar stool. "Come on. I'll buy you some more ginger ale, too. And don't pee until I get back!"

Olivia didn't sit down again while waiting for Samantha. She paced from the living room to the hallway to Samantha's bedroom, and then back again, and then again. The longer Samantha was gone, the more her hope built. And damn it, that was bad. Hope was dangerous. Hope made you want something before you knew if you could have it.

So, for nearly forty-five excruciating minutes, she paced and hoped and told herself not to hope and paced some more. When Samantha finally rushed in with a bag in one hand and a six-pack of ginger ale in the other, Olivia had worked herself up to the point that hope was bubbling and percolating through her veins, leaving her unable to speak.

"I'm so sorry it took so long!" Sam reached into the bag and took out three boxes. "There were tons of people at the store. The cashier was incredibly slow, and one guy's credit card didn't go through, and—" She broke off. "Doesn't matter. Here. I bought three brands. So, you know, you can see if all three give the same result."

Olivia stared at Samantha and fought to stay rational. "What if I'm not?"

Samantha blinked. "Most women, when faced with a potential unplanned pregnancy wouldn't ask that question, my dear. They would be asking 'What if I am?'" She stepped forward and held out the pregnancy kits. With a knowing smile, she said, "Just something to think about, Olivia."

Accepting the three boxes, Olivia turned on her heel to go the bathroom. Stopped. Turned back around. "Don't they say you should take the test in the morning? For the best results?"

"I bought two of each of kind." Sam shook the still-full bag. "If those come up negative, you can retest in the morning. But these tests are ultrasensitive now. You might as well see."

Fate, Olivia soon discovered, can slip in a few surprises when you're least prepared. Not all of them were bad. Not all of them stole something precious from you. Sometimes, something precious was *given* to you. She stared at the three pregnancy tests packaged in three slightly different ways, and her hope turned to reality. All three were positive.

She was going to have a baby. Grady's baby. *Their* baby.

Chapter Twelve

Five days before Christmas, and not one word from Olivia. Granted, Grady hadn't contacted her, either. But that was because he'd sworn to himself to give her the time she needed. Well, a little time, anyway. He'd already decided if she hadn't called him by Christmas Day, he'd at least check in. Not to pressure her, but to wish her a merry Christmas and to give her a gift he'd been saving. He believed with every cell in his body that she was finally ready to receive it. Hopefully, he was right in that belief.

Stepping out of the shower, he toweled off and tried to decide how he would spend the long day ahead. He supposed he could do more shopping, but he'd already bought something for everyone on his list. And even though he'd closed the shop for the week, he could go in and get some work done on the Corvette that had come in the prior week. Or he could head over to Jace's and give him a hand with his house's renovation. Something he'd been promising to do for well over a month, but hadn't gotten around to. As a bonus, he could badger his brother about Melanie. See how that Secret Santa move paid off.

The truth was, though, that Grady didn't particularly want to do any of those things. He ached to see Olivia. To hold her. To laugh with her. Hell, he'd be content to simply sit and stare at her for a while.

"Pitiful," he muttered. "She may very well choose to live her life without you. What are you going to do, spend the rest of your days pining for her?"

Maybe. Probably.

Okay. Jace's it was, then. Grady put on his jeans and sweatshirt and went to give his brother a call. The phone rang the second his hand reached for it. Instinct sent a chill straight through him and his damn knees buckled. A glance at the Caller ID had his heart racing and acid sloshing around in his stomach. Olivia. *Finally.*

The phone rang again. He hesitated, somehow afraid to answer the call he'd been waiting eight endless days for. "Wake up, man," he said when the phone rang for a third time. A hundred and ninety-two hours of dead silence and he was standing here like an idiot. Not just any old type of idiot, either. But a shivering, weak-kneed, cold-palmed, fluttering-heart idiot at that. Not cool.

He jabbed the answer button. "Hello?" he barked into the phone.

"Umm…Grady?" Olivia said, the sound of her voice seeping over him like a salve on a fresh burn. "Are you all right? Is this a bad time for you to talk?"

He tried to answer, but his vocal cords felt as if they were covered in a thick, gluey paste. So, instead of the "Now is fine" he meant to say, what came out was, "Nowth ith thine."

"Are you drunk, Grady?" Olivia asked. "At nine on a Tuesday morning?"

Damn it. His gaze swept the room, looking for something to drink. Nothing. He took off for the kitchen. Fast. And managed to run straight into the wall.

"Grady? What was that noise?" Olivia's concern filtered through the line loud and clear.

Water. He needed water. Making it to the kitchen he turned on the faucet full blast, filled a glass with water, and drank it down. "Sorry, Olly." Whew. He sounded somewhat normal. "I…umm…had food in my mouth. And then dropped the phone. All's good now."

"There you are. Jeez, you had me worried."

He pulled a chair out and sat down. "I'm fine," he assured her. "How are you?"

She sighed the slightest of sighs. "I'm good. I'm sorry I haven't called before now. That wasn't very fair of me, but…well, I needed to put some stuff in order."

"I told you to take all the time you needed. I meant that." Even if he'd almost died from the waiting. "What… umm…can I do for you?"

"Well, I was looking at the Christmas tree this morning and realized I left that beautiful ornament you gave me in your truck. I…hope it didn't break or get lost or anything."

She was calling about the snowflake? The heavy weight of disappointment replaced his relief at hearing from her. "The ornament is fine, Olly. I have it right here, hanging in the kitchen window."

"Okay, good." She paused, and he could almost see her pacing as she contemplated on what to say next. "Well, I was hoping… What I mean to say is—would you like to come over on Christmas Eve? You…can bring the ornament with you. I love it so much, and I'd like to hang it on the tree while you're here."

"Christmas Eve?" he half gurgled, half whimpered.

"Do you have other plans? I know you'll be at your folks' house on Christmas Day, but I thought… Well, maybe we can get together after Christmas, then?"

"No plans!" he shouted. God, what the hell was wrong with him? "Yes, Olly. I would very much enjoy spending Christmas Eve with you. What time were you thinking?"

"Seven?"

"Sure! Seven." Kind of early, but maybe that was a good sign? Perhaps she wanted to spend the entire day with him? "Okay. Want me to bring anything for breakfast?"

"Er, Grady…I meant seven at night," she said with a small laugh. "Are you sure you haven't been drinking? You're very exuberant this morning."

"Not drinking. Just heading out the door to help Jace," he said slowly, enunciating each word carefully. "So… umm…kind of in a hurry. But seven in the evening is fine." *Better.* At least he hadn't shouted in her ear.

"Oh," she said. Was that disappointment he heard? "You should get going, then. I'll see you on Christmas Eve. Tell Jace I said hi."

He moved his jaw up and down to make sure it was functioning. Then, "Will do! See you then, Olivia." As soon as he heard her disconnect, he threw the phone on the floor and groaned.

Loudly.

"Welcome to a repeat of your adolescence," he muttered. "As if once wasn't enough."

Combing his fingers through his hair, he replayed the entire conversation. Yeah, he'd been on the wrong side of crazy throughout the whole damn thing. Even when he'd originally met Olivia, he hadn't succumbed to that level of idiocy.

But she had called. And she wanted to see him. On Christmas Eve, no less. He couldn't imagine the Olivia he knew ending their marriage on a holiday. Throughout everything, she had never been cruel. So should he feel hopeful? Maybe. But he didn't.

He was just too damn scared.

"Heya, Cody," Olivia said early Christmas Eve afternoon. She was sitting on her son's bed in his brightly painted bedroom. "I know we talked yesterday, when I visited you at the cemetery, but I… Well, I guess I just have more to say."

Jasper vaulted onto the bed and shoved his body against Olivia's hand, begging to be loved. She acquiesced to the cat and rubbed her knuckles along his back.

"Jasper misses you, too, baby. Everyone does. Yesterday, I told you how much I love you, but I neglected to thank you. You see, Cody, I've been so lost in my grief over missing you, that I'd forgotten how amazing of a kid you were."

Tears filled her eyes and spilled down the sides of her face. She didn't wipe them away. She took comfort in them. She treasured them. She honored them. For who they fell for, for what they represented.

"Being your mom taught me so much about life. The way you'd delight in a sunny day, or get excited about the birds who sang in the trees—" she pointed out Cody's bedroom windows "—right out there, and how you loved the way Jasper would curl up and sleep with you. You saw miracles everywhere you looked, and then, you shared them with me…with your dad."

She had to stop to take a breath, to let the ache in her

throat soften enough she could speak again. When it did, she continued, "Mommy kind of forgot all that stuff, Cody. And that made it hard for me to find happiness anywhere. I forgot to be thankful for all the little miracles in life, all the things you knew instinctively were special. But recently, I began to remember."

Heavy, rumbling purrs erupted from Jasper. He stood on her lap and pushed his head against the underside of her chin. "Yes, yes, Jasper. I know you're here." He instantly settled on her lap. Then, just like she had that night with Grady, she fisted her hand and pressed it against her chest.

"I'm not going to lie. Losing you is the greatest hurt of my life. I will always wish you were here with us. I will never stop yearning to see your smile or hear your laugh or feel you in my arms. You were my baby." The tears poured now, heavy and relentless. "You will always be my baby. My boy."

Again, she had to pause to get her bearings, to find the right words. Jasper rolled over on his back and worked his paws against her shirt. She tickled his belly, somehow finding the motion calming. And, like Karen had said on Thanksgiving about the tea, soothing. To her heart, to her soul, to the raw ache deep, deep inside.

"So, my son," Olivia said softly, "Thank you for every gift you ever gave me, for everything you ever showed me, for every laugh and every hug and every precious second you were here. You have changed me forever. I am a better person because of you. And, God, I so hope you can hear me, somehow, but Cody Jonathon Foster, I swear to you that I will never forget any of this ever again."

Breathe, she instructed herself, *just breathe.*

Once she was calmer, she picked Jasper up in her arms and stood. She hadn't yet stopped crying, but she would.

And while she knew the tears would come again, and that the aching loss of Cody would never completely disappear, she also knew that she was ready...so very ready... to live life again. For her son. For her unborn child. For her husband—if he'd still have her. But mostly, for herself.

"Goodbye for now, kiddo. I need to get ready for your dad. I have a very special Christmas planned for us."

As she left Cody's bedroom, she felt something—a stirring of the soul, a whisper in her heart—that made her turn around. There was nothing to see that she hadn't already seen, but she felt sure that her son had, indeed, heard her.

"Merry Christmas, baby," she whispered.

Olivia waited impatiently for Grady to show. Why had she decided on seven o'clock? She should have had him come over at the crack of dawn. Last night. Three days ago. Heck, the very second she'd made her decision. But she so wanted this to be special, and what could be more special than Christmas Eve?

More than that, though, there were steps she absolutely needed to take before moving forward. She needed to prove to herself that she truly was strong enough to enter life again, to be the wife that Grady deserved, to be the person that she wanted to be. Basically, a fully functioning human being. And yes, those elements took her longer than she'd have liked.

But she'd done them, every last one, and now...now she wanted Grady to get here. Nervous, she stalked to the window, but resisted temptation to peer out at her driveway again. Instead, she released some of her pent-up energy by pacing the area around the coffee table. Basically, she walked in circles. One after the other. Over and over.

What if he'd decided she'd waited too long? What if, upon reflection, he'd decided that his life would be simpler without her? If he'd reached that conclusion in the thirteen odd days since she'd last seen him, she wouldn't—couldn't—fault him. And he had sounded rather odd when she'd phoned him earlier in the week. So what did that mean?

Okay. She was going to make herself crazy.

Obviously, though, these questions required an answer before she told him about the baby. Grady had such honor, such a strong belief in family, that he'd stay married to her despite what he felt. Despite what decision he might have reached.

She stopped pacing midcircle and gave in to temptation. Pushing the curtain away from the living room window for what had to be the thousandth time, she searched for his headlights. Nope. Not yet. A glance at the clock showed she had another ten minutes or so to wait, and knowing Grady's penchant for punctuality, he wouldn't arrive even a minute sooner than seven. Or, for that matter, one minute later.

"You can get through ten minutes," she said to the window. Fortunately, the window didn't respond. Shaking her head in frustrated humor, she started to step away from the curtain when she heard the distinctive rumble of Grady's truck. He was here. Early, even. Grady was never early for anything. Good sign or bad sign?

She ran to the hall mirror for one last once-over. Well, she looked the same as she had the other ten times she'd checked. Then, she closed her eyes, breathed and waited for the doorbell to ring. "One Mississippi, two Mississippi, three Mississippi, four Mississippi," she whispered. "Five Mississippi, six Mississippi, seven Miss—" The loud peal

of the bell sent her heart into overdrive before it plum-
meted into her stomach.

Her palm was damp enough that it slid on the doorknob, but she managed to get a good enough grip to open
the door. And there he was. Tall. Handsome. Solid. "Hi,
Grady," she said, swinging the door open wider. Wow.
She actually sounded as if she had it together. As if she
hadn't just been running around in circles and stalking a
pane of glass.

"Merry Christmas, Olivia," Grady said, entering the
foyer. He held a bag in each hand. Offering one to her, he
said, "Mom baked some cookies. She wanted you to have
them."

"That's sweet. I'll have to call her with my thanks."
Accepting them, she gestured to the living room. "Go
on in. Sit down. I...I'll be right back." She was halfway
to the kitchen before she remembered her manners. "Oh!
Would you like something to drink? Are you hungry?"

He gave her an odd look and shook his head. "I couldn't
eat or drink anything right now."

Right. She continued to the kitchen and put the container of cookies on the counter. *Wait! What did that
mean?* Maybe he couldn't eat or drink because he knew
he was about to deliver bad news? Or, her silently optimistic side pointed out, maybe he was nervous because
he worried he was going to *get* bad news.

For whatever reason, that thought strengthened her.
Gave her conviction enough to calm her nerves and ease
the roiling in her stomach. This was a good day. This was
a day where anything could happen. A day where her
dreams could come true.

Holding her head high, she retraced her steps to the living room. Grady was standing near the tree, fingering the
picture ornament of Cody and the snowman. She stood

quietly, not wanting to interrupt her husband's moment, but also so she could take a mental snapshot to remember the way he looked, with his black hair tousled around his face and his expression quietly contemplative. Wow. She loved him so much.

"Grady," she said softly. "I am so happy to see you."

Warmth and hope replaced the contemplation. "I'm glad to be here."

"I've… There are… We need to have a conversation. I don't want to beat around the bush or pretend I'm not crazy nervous." She took one step toward him. "And I see no reason to put this off any longer. Of making you wait any longer."

Grady closed his eyes for the briefest of seconds. His shoulders straightened and his jaw tightened. "So it's time, is it?" He went to the couch and sat down quickly, almost as if he worried his legs wouldn't support him. She felt the same way about hers. Holding his hand out, he said, "Sit with me, Olly. I'd prefer to have you here, rather than over there on the opposite side of the room while we have this conversation."

"Okay. Sure." She tried to walk, but found she couldn't. "Yep. I can sit there. By you. No problem." What was going on? The man she loved was asking her to sit next to him, and her stupid legs refused to move.

He gave her the smallest of smiles. "I won't bite, sweetheart."

"I'll be right there. Just as soon as I can…" Oh, to hell with it. "I'm over here because I can't walk at the moment, Grady." But then, as soon as the words were said, she *could* move. So she did, before her legs decided to turn to stone again. She sighed in relief when she reached the sofa and collapsed onto it. "Never mind," she said brightly. "I'm here."

"So I see. You said you had something to tell me?"

"Yes!" Way too loud. She tried again, "I… Jeez, Grady. There are so many things I need to say, and I can't figure out what to say first."

"Look at me." His tenor was calm and stable. Olivia lifted her chin and settled her gaze on his. *Yes.* So much better. "And say the first thing that pops into your head."

"I'm seeing a grief counselor," she blurted. Not exactly where she'd meant to start, but it would do okay as an opening.

Surprise darted over Grady's features, and perhaps a whisper of relief. "Really? I… That's good, right?"

She nodded. "I've only seen her twice so far, but I plan on continuing. I'm learning a lot about why I…why I pushed you and everyone else away." Her courage grew by a minuscule amount, fueling the rest of her words. "I doubt I will ever feel comfortable at your bereavement group, but if it's important to you, I'm willing to try. I mean that, with all of my heart."

"I don't care if you ever go to that group. I wanted to find a way to help you, and I was drawing straws as to what might work." He regarded her with serious eyes. "But I was wrong in the way I went about trying to help you. I'm glad you've found something that is helping you, something that you believe will be successful. All I hope for is your happiness."

Inch by inch, her muscles began to relax. "I know that, Grady. Even when I was angry, I knew that." Her fingers fluttered in her lap, her desire to touch him was so strong. She resisted. "I've also been thinking a lot about Cody. Remembering him and everything he was to us."

"He was our world," Grady said. "Our entire lives revolved around him."

"Yes. I guess that's a big part of why I had such difficulty talking about him, and I'm so sorry about that. You were right, that morning in your apartment. We *should* talk about him. That's how we can keep him with us, how we can show our love for him."

Gathering her hands in his, Grady said quietly, "One of the hardest yet happiest days of this past month was decorating the Christmas tree with you and sharing memories of our son. I can't tell you how much that day meant to me."

"You don't have to. I already know." The mention of the tree reminded her of Cody's presents. She sighed. Might as well get everything out there before her courage deserted her.

"I take it there's more you have to say?" Ah, and there was that pensive worry again, etched into his face.

"There is. The reason I asked about Cody's gifts is because I decided to donate them to charity." Twisting her fingers together, she continued, "Next year, I might try buying new gifts, but this year…I wasn't there yet. I should have waited for you. I'm sorry I didn't."

Grady was silent for a minute. Maybe two. His contemplative expression returned. "This entire conversation is taking me by surprise one word at a time."

"Are you upset that I didn't wait?"

"Not at all. I'm proud of you, Olly." Suddenly, he ran his hands over his eyes. "I feel like I'm missing something here. Everything you've said is wonderful, sweetheart. But…why do you look so anxious? What is it that you don't want to put off any longer?"

"That would be this." Ignoring the shivering chill of worry trickling down her neck, she reached over to the end table and grabbed the manila envelope she'd left there earlier. Offering it to Grady, she said, "This is for you. It's probably best if you review it now."

He looked at the envelope as if it were a monster from the depths of hell. "So you have decided?"

"I have." Stay calm, she told herself. Hope for the best, be ready for the worst.

"I take it those are the divorce papers?"

She held her eyes as wide open as possible. "Look and see."

Quicker than a wink, he rose to his feet. He took the envelope and shoved it between his arm and his side. "I'll have these taken care of as soon as the holiday is over."

"We're not done, Grady," she said. "Sit down, please."

"Why? Is there a point?" Frustration rippled over him like waves of heat in the middle of July. "I said you can have anything you want. There is no need for me to go over this now. Not in front of the Christmas tree on Christmas Eve."

"Yes, there is. It's extremely important that we review this document together. Now."

Something in her expression caused his eyebrows to bunch together. He sort of fell, sort of toppled back to the couch. "Why? Just tell me why, Olly. What could I have done different, or what did I do wrong?"

"Please, Grady. Open the envelope. Once you do, I'll tell you anything you want to hear."

"Fine," he said in a curt voice. He tore the top off of the envelope rather than simply unclasping it. She held her breath while he tugged out the single sheet of paper she'd written on. And hoped with every part of who she was. "What is this, Olly?"

"You're such a stubborn man, Grady Foster," she said. "I love you. So very much. That letter is my promise to you to never give up on our marriage again." She prayed that he wanted her. That it wasn't too late. "There's even a place for our signatures at the bottom."

Relief, palpable and swift, eased the harsh edge of his shoulders and the unforgiving line of his jaw. "This isn't about the divorce?"

"I don't want a divorce," she said in a near-whisper. "I want you. I want our life. I'm hoping that you still want me."

"Hoping *I* still want you?" He tipped his head back and laughed. "God, Olly. You just about gave me a heart attack. I thought…I thought you were kicking me to the curb with my tail between my legs. Why this way? You could've leapt into my arms the second I walked in the door…why the subterfuge?"

"I was afraid," she admitted, very aware that he hadn't yet said he wanted her, that he loved her. "That you would say you'd wasted enough time on me. I…I don't know. Writing that agreement felt safer. Plus, I sort of owed you one."

"Ah, yes. The deal." Grady leaned against the couch, his shoulders relaxed. "Point taken. You definitely owed me one."

"Two, actually. Seeing how Samantha is the one who clued you in on joint property." Not that Olivia had cared by the time Sam confessed. In fact, she'd hugged her friend as hard as she could and thanked her for butting in. Oh, and apologized for calling her a crackpot.

"You love me?" he asked, everything in his voice and on his face asking for confirmation. "And you are in this marriage. *Our* marriage. For real?"

"I love you," she said, looking directly into his eyes. "And I am in this marriage. For real. For better or worse. Forever."

"Sweetheart, you sure know how to keep a man guessing. I didn't know if this day would ever come. If you'd… Baby, you are worth every single minute I've waited." His tone lowered to that sexy, husky drawl that turned Olivia to mush. "I'd wait longer to feel like this. To be with you, I would wait forever."

"You shouldn't have had to wait for so long." She took in a deep breath. Tingles sped along her skin, making her shiver in disbelief...in happiness...that this was really happening. But it wasn't complete. Not yet. "There's more," she whispered, on the edge of her seat with the miracle she was about to share with Grady. "So much more that you don't know. I have a very special Christmas gift for you. You see—"

"Wait. If we're unwrapping presents, I have one that I'd like you to open first."

"But you'll want this present, Grady. And I'm so excited to—"

"Please, Olivia," he said, his gaze searching and earnest. "I've been waiting a really long time to give you this. And I think...I feel that you need this now. Right here, beside this beautiful tree. By Cody's tree. Please?"

Well, she couldn't object to that, could she? Besides, he'd made her awfully curious. And a little apprehensive, though she couldn't say why. "Okay. You win. You can go first."

He reached for the other bag he'd walked in the door with. "Well, first, you should have this," he said as he pulled out her snowflake ornament. "We definitely want that on the tree. In fact—" he scooted over to the floor "—let's sit by the tree, shall we? Right here next to Cody's picture."

"Sure..." What was he up to? She sat across from him and accepted the crystal snowflake. With care, she suspended the ornament from a branch barely above her head. "There, it's perfect, isn't it? And look...I knew the lights would make it even more beautiful."

"Not more beautiful than you." Then, all at once, his demeanor changed from jubilant to somber. Wistful, even. Her stomach cramped as a new bout of worry crawled in.

"What's wrong, Grady?"

"Nothing, sweetheart. I promise," he said in a raw, ragged sort of way. "But I have a present in this bag. For you from Cody. It's—" He stopped speaking abruptly, as if trying to get a grip on his emotions. "It's from the year he died, sweetheart. I've been holding on to this, waiting until you were ready, waiting until the day I could give this to you."

Her chin trembled in shock, in emotion, in wondrous disbelief. Yes, her son had definitely heard her this morning. And now... "You have a gift for me from Cody?"

"Yes. Would you like to open it?"

There was no hesitation, no doubt, just a sweet exhilaration that overrode all else. "Yes, Grady. Very much so."

Grady reached into the bag and pulled out a small box that was clumsily wrapped in reindeer paper. He placed the gift gently in her lap. "For you," he said simply.

Her gaze dropped to the present wrapped by her son's hands. A tag was taped to the top that said, "To Mommy, From Cody." At the bottom of the tag was one row of *X*s and *O*s. Hugs and kisses from her baby.

A tiny sob curled in the back of her throat and a tremble whisked through her body. She slowly picked off the five layers of tape her son had used to seal the wrapping paper. She laughed through her tears when she saw the box. He'd colored the entirety of it with red, blue and green crayons.

"Cody must have thought plain white was too plain, huh?" she said quietly, looking at her husband. "Always the artist."

There were tears in Grady's eyes, too. But he nodded and gestured for her to continue. So, she slowly removed the lid and pulled out the top, thick cotton layer to reveal what lay beneath. Her heart blew up like a huge, overfilled balloon, and her trembles turned to shivers. Goose bumps rode her arms, her back, her legs.

"Oh, Grady. Oh…" She couldn't talk anymore then. Not when she was crying so very hard. Harder than she ever had before, possibly. For her son—likely with his father's help—had given her a gold necklace with three charms suspended on the fragile chain. Three tiny gold figures: a mommy, a daddy and a little boy. And the faces of each figure were the birthstones for the person they represented.

Now she understood why Grady had waited to give this precious gift to her. This would've hurt her too much before now—before today—for her to find any pleasure in receiving it, in wearing it. But now…now, this necklace, the colored box it came in and the tag addressed to her was a miracle. Pure and simple. A miracle from Cody.

"This is so beautiful." She lifted the necklace out of the box. "Will you help me put it on?" she asked her husband. "Please?"

"Of course." Grady gently removed the necklace from her grip and unclasped it. "Lift your hair, sweetheart." She swiveled around and did as he asked. His warm fingers brushed against the base of her neck as he fastened the necklace. "There you go."

With her hand clutching the three figures resting against her skin, she turned to look at the picture of her son. He stood there with his snowman, proud and smiling. Mischievous brown eyes filled with light and happiness stared back at her. "Thank you for my gift, Cody. I love the necklace, baby."

"You okay?" Grady asked, stroking her hair off of her tear-streaked face. "This is good, right? You're happy, right?"

"This is very good." She pulled the necklace away from her neck, so the chain was taut and fingered the charms. "There is a problem, though," she said lightly, her heart cracking with the want to share her news with her husband. "We'll need to buy another one of these in August, for when the baby comes. Do you know the birthstone for August, Grady?"

"Peridot," he replied instantly. She counted to five before his hand stilled. Before what she'd said made an impact. His voice, gruff and disbelieving, but so filled with hope that she could feel it sparkling in the air, whispered into her ears. "What did you say, Olly?"

She touched his hair, his cheek, his lips and the very strong line of his jaw. "We're having a baby, my love. In August."

Grady's face crinkled into myriad lines. His jaw worked as he tried to talk, but she didn't need to hear his words. She saw the strength of his emotions in his eyes. And like before, they mirrored hers. This time, though, on this day, that emotion was sweet, pure joy.

"I love you," he said. "I have always loved you, Olivia."

"And I will always love you," she said. "Merry Christmas, Grady."

His mouth found hers in a deep, smoldering kiss that seemed to last an eternity. A kiss that she felt to her toes. A kiss that spoke of their past, their present and their future. Happily ever after, she decided as her husband carried her upstairs to their bedroom, was a state of mind, a meeting of hearts and a joining of souls.

And Lord, did she have all three of those in spades.

Epilogue

Olivia woke in the early hours of Christmas morning with Grady's arms wrapped securely around her and a warm, purring ball of cat wedged against her chest. Outside their bedroom window, snow fell in a lazy hushed whisper that, once again, made her believe in magic. In miracles.

If Cody were here, he'd have had them awake hours ago. The presents would likely already be opened, and she'd be preparing breakfast. Grady, she thought with a smile, would be peering over an instruction manual for one of Cody's new toys. A few hours later, they'd be on their way to John and Karen's, where there would be more presents to open and more instruction manuals to make sense of. There would be laughter and love, family and togetherness.

Olivia sighed, snuggled closer to her husband, and waited for the familiar ache of loss to gather beneath her breastbone, for the anger of her life being forever altered by a twist of fate to sweep in. She closed her eyes and pictured Cody's face, his smile. She heard his voice in her mind, as fluttery and whispery as the snow falling outside.

Yes, the ache was there. A dull, throbbing sensation that would probably never leave completely, but there was also joy in remembering her son. And the anger, she was surprised to find, had vanished, replaced by a sweet surety that her life still had meaning and that her future could be filled with happiness.

Today truly was the first day of the rest of her life. A life she'd share with Grady, with the child growing inside of her, and possibly more children down the line. One Christmas from now...just one...there would be a child in this house again. The thought was startling and wondrous and...there was that word again—*miraculous*—all at once.

What better time to begin this new chapter of their lives than on Christmas Day, with their family surrounding them? That thought put an idea into her head, and the more she considered it, the more she liked it. Today should have meaning. Today should be a true beginning for her, for Grady, for everyone who loved them and had been rooting for them all along.

Carefully, so she wouldn't wake Grady or disturb the cat, Olivia slid out of her husband's hold and crawled to the end of the bed. Memories, whether good or bad, stayed with you—in one form or another—forever. And she wanted to create a memory for today, for this Christmas, that she and Grady would cherish for the rest of their lives.

She silently made her way to the kitchen, where she dialed her mother-in-law's number first, knowing that

Karen and John would be thrilled to jump on board. Next was Samantha, and then, even though Olivia knew she'd wake him, she phoned Jace. Seth couldn't be with them, but maybe they'd be able to talk to him at some point during the day. And her parents were celebrating the holidays in Europe, so there was no reason to contact them.

When the phone calls were complete, Olivia started a pot of coffee before floating to the shower. She couldn't wait to surprise Grady with what she had planned.

Yes, today was going to be one hell of a memory.

Olivia could just see the top of Grady's head from her place at the head of the staircase, and she knew he was waiting for her with as much nervous anticipation as she felt. Silly, really, when she was already married to this man, when she'd already spent so many years loving him. Somehow, though, today was different from the first time they'd exchanged vows.

She knew more now, she supposed. Understood more about herself and Grady, about marriage. About how precious life was and how quickly it could change. Yes, she was a stronger, wiser woman today than the innocent girl who'd stepped onto the aisle so long ago.

And this woman wanted—no, *needed*—to repledge her love and devotion to the man who'd never given up on her or their marriage.

Her father-in-law came to the bottom of the stairs and motioned for her to join him. "It's time," he said softly. "Everyone is here, and Grady has that flustered look he gets whenever he's in a suit. Pretty sure the boy is about to rip off his tie if you keep him waiting much longer."

Olivia nodded, ran her palms down the sides of the slinky red dress she'd bought on a whim last week. A dress that was nothing like the formal princess gown with the train that went on forever she'd worn during their original ceremony, but that was okay. She didn't want to replicate the past. Besides which, she felt *good* in this dress. Luscious and alive and joyful.

She took the steps slowly until she met up with John. He gave her that twinkly eyed smile and crooked his arm. "You're quite the picture, Olivia. Beautiful in every way."

"I feel beautiful. Thank you. For being here, for welcoming me back into the family. For…well, everything."

"What do you mean back into the family? The way I see it, you never left." His voice turned gruff for a moment. "You needed some time, that's all."

"Maybe you're right," Olivia agreed, slipping her arm through his. "But now…now I don't want to waste another second."

"Then let's get this show on the road."

Together, they walked the few short steps into the living room. The Christmas tree was ablaze with twinkling lights, soft music played in the background, the snow continued to dance in the air outside the window and the room was filled with the people she loved.

Well, most of the people she loved.

Karen and Samantha were off to the side, standing near the sofa. Jace stood with his back to the Christmas tree, a single sheet of paper in his hand. And Grady—her handsome, solid, sexy husband—had planted himself in front of Jace, but his body was angled toward her. Out of the three suits he owned, he'd chosen the black one, which he'd paired with a red tie. She wondered briefly if someone had clued him in on the color of her dress, or if his choice was simply one of those rare moments of serendipity.

His gaze raked down her body and back up. His lips curved into a smile and his cinnamon eyes darkened in desire, in love. Within those eyes, she saw forever.

A few more steps brought her to him. "Hey, there," she said, barely noticing when John released her arm and placed her hand in Grady's. "I—"

Her words were cut off when Grady pulled her tight to him and met her lips with his. The somersaults in her stomach disappeared beneath the weight of her want as he deepened the kiss, as his fingers combed into the back of her hair, pulling her even closer. Heat tumbled through her body, quick and fierce and all-encompassing.

Jace cleared his throat. "If memory serves me correctly, the kiss comes later. I printed out the vows and... Okay, they're not listening to me. At all."

Grady ignored his brother and continued his slow exploration of her mouth, almost as if he'd never kissed her before. His hands slid down her back and a moan gurgled from her throat. She forgot where she was, who was there with them, why they were even there. She forgot everything but the feel of Grady's mouth, of the sensations his kiss evoked.

Until, that is, light laughter came from behind. Samantha's throaty chuckle came first, followed by Karen's. John coughed and Jace whistled a tune that Olivia didn't recognize.

"Should we leave you two lovebirds alone?" Jace asked. "Or...are you going to come up for air anytime soon?"

Olivia lightly pressed on Grady's chest to break the kiss. "No, don't leave." To Grady, she said, "This is important to me. There are things I want to say to you, in front of our family."

His expression became serious and he nodded. "Whatever you need, sweetheart. But, baby, none of this is necessary for me. We're together. That's all I care about."

She centered herself by grasping on to Grady's hands. "I know. But I want everyone in this room to know what

I told you last night. That I love you. That I promise to never give up on our marriage again. That I am so sorry for turning away when you needed me the most." Her voice hitched, so she breathed in deeply before continuing. "I have never known a man like you, Grady Foster. You never doubted me, my love for you, or your love for me. You never stopped believing that we could make this work. Even…even when I did."

"Like I said last night—you're worth every minute I waited." With a quick shake of his head and the tiniest bit of frustration in his voice, he said, "Don't you get it, Olly? What I feel for you…it's every sappy love song put together. It's the stars and the moon and the way the air smells after the rain. It's… You give me the strength. *You* make me the man I am."

Oh. Wow. Tears blinded her vision, so she blinked. How had she been so lucky to have this amazing man fall in love with her? Forgetting the traditional vows she'd planned on reciting, she tipped her chin up so she could look directly into her husband's eyes. "I do, Grady. I will. Beginning now, for every second of every day, I'm yours."

Grady closed the gap between them. He lightly stroked his thumb along the curve of her cheek. "And I'm yours. That will never change."

"This is what I wanted," Olivia said quietly. "I wanted this moment for us to have. Not in replacement of our wedding, but as an…addendum, I guess. Something to mark the end of the darkest days and the beginning of whatever is ahead of us."

Jace cleared his throat again. "Right. I guess this is when I, being the unofficial officiator who didn't officiate in the least, declare you as husband and wife. Now, you may kiss the bride!"

There was whooping and cheering and clapping all

around them as Grady cupped her cheeks with his hands. He leaned over, whispered, "I love you" and then brushed her lips in a soft, sweet kiss that held the promise of more to come. Later. When they were alone and could devote hours upon hours to each other.

Olivia couldn't wait until they were alone. They had a lot of time to make up for.

After they separated, Jace, who was still playing the officiator role, said, "I present Mr. and Mrs. Grady Foster. Aren't they a lovely couple?"

"Don't forget Baby Foster," Grady supplied with a wide grin and a protective pat on Olivia's still-flat belly. "But he or she won't be making his or her official appearance until sometime in August."

That was when the real cheering began, along with more than a few tears being shed. Jace tried to pretend he had something stuck in his eye, but Olivia knew better.

Hours later, after all the presents were opened, too many cookies consumed, and everyone had gone home, Olivia found Grady in the living room in front of the Christmas tree. By Cody's tree. As before, Dean Martin was singing "Silent Night."

Hearing her, Grady turned and held out his hand. "Come here, sweetheart."

She did. And then, with her cheek on her husband's chest, they danced. In celebration of the son they would always and forever cherish, of their love for each other and for the future that awaited them.

* * * * *

HEART & HOME

Heartwarming romances where love can happen right when you least expect it.

Harlequin®
SPECIAL EDITION®

COMING NEXT MONTH
AVAILABLE NOVEMBER 22, 2011

#2155 TRUE BLUE
Diana Palmer

#2156 HER MONTANA CHRISTMAS GROOM
Montana Mavericks: The Texans Are Coming!
Teresa Southwick

#2157 ALMOST A CHRISTMAS BRIDE
Wives for Hire
Susan Crosby

#2158 A BABY UNDER THE TREE
Brighton Valley Babies
Judy Duarte

#2159 CHRISTMAS WITH THE MUSTANG MAN
Men of the West
Stella Bagwell

#2160 ROYAL HOLIDAY BRIDE
Reigning Men
Brenda Harlen

You can find more information on upcoming Harlequin® titles, free excerpts and more at www.HarlequinInsideRomance.com.

HSECNM1111

REQUEST YOUR FREE BOOKS!

2 FREE NOVELS PLUS 2 FREE GIFTS!

♦ Harlequin®

SPECIAL EDITION

Life, Love & Family

YES! Please send me 2 FREE Harlequin® Special Edition novels and my 2 FREE gifts (gifts are worth about $10). After receiving them, if I don't wish to receive any more books, I can return the shipping statement marked "cancel." If I don't cancel, I will receive 6 brand-new novels every month and be billed just $4.49 per book in the U.S. or $5.24 per book in Canada. That's a saving of at least 14% off the cover price! It's quite a bargain! Shipping and handling is just 50¢ per book in the U.S. and 75¢ per book in Canada.* I understand that accepting the 2 free books and gifts places me under no obligation to buy anything. I can always return a shipment and cancel at any time. Even if I never buy another book, the two free books and gifts are mine to keep forever.

235/335 HDN FEGF

Name	(PLEASE PRINT)	
Address		Apt. #
City	State/Prov.	Zip/Postal Code

Signature (if under 18, a parent or guardian must sign)

Mail to the **Reader Service:**
IN U.S.A.: P.O. Box 1867, Buffalo, NY 14240-1867
IN CANADA: P.O. Box 609, Fort Erie, Ontario L2A 5X3

Not valid for current subscribers to Harlequin Special Edition books.

Want to try two free books from another line?
Call 1-800-873-8635 or visit www.ReaderService.com.

* Terms and prices subject to change without notice. Prices do not include applicable taxes. Sales tax applicable in N.Y. Canadian residents will be charged applicable taxes. Offer not valid in Quebec. This offer is limited to one order per household. All orders subject to credit approval. Credit or debit balances in a customer's account(s) may be offset by any other outstanding balance owed by or to the customer. Please allow 4 to 6 weeks for delivery. Offer available while quantities last.

Your Privacy—The Reader Service is committed to protecting your privacy. Our Privacy Policy is available online at www.ReaderService.com or upon request from the Reader Service.

We make a portion of our mailing list available to reputable third parties that offer products we believe may interest you. If you prefer that we not exchange your name with third parties, or if you wish to clarify or modify your communication preferences, please visit us at www.ReaderService.com/consumerschoice or write to us at Reader Service Preference Service, P.O. Box 9062, Buffalo, NY 14269. Include your complete name and address.

HSE11B

Lucy Flemming and Ross Mitchell shared a magical,
sexy Christmas weekend together six years ago.
This Christmas, history may repeat itself when they find
themselves stranded in a major snowstorm...
and alone at last.

Read on for a sneak peek from
IT HAPPENED ONE CHRISTMAS
by Leslie Kelly.

Available December 2011, only from Harlequin® Blaze™.

EYEING THE GRAY, THICK SKY through the expansive wall of
windows, Lucy began to pack up her photography gear.
The Christmas party was winding down, only a dozen or so
people remaining on this floor, which had been transformed
from cubicles and meeting rooms to a holiday funland. She
smiled at those nearest to her, then, seeing the glances at her
silly elf hat, she reached up to tug it off her head.

Before she could do it, however, she heard a voice. A
deep, male voice—smooth and sexy, and so not Santa's.

"I appreciate you filling in on such short notice. I've
heard you do a terrific job."

Lucy didn't turn around, letting her brain process what
she was hearing. Her whole body had stiffened, the hairs on
the back of her neck standing up, her skin tightening into
tiny goose bumps. Because that voice sounded so familiar.
Impossibly familiar.

It can't be.

"It sounds like the kids had a great time."

Unable to stop herself, Lucy began to turn around,
wondering if her ears—and all her other senses—were
deceiving her. After all, six years was a long time, the mind

could play tricks. What were the odds that she'd bump into *him,* here? And today of all days. December 23.

Six years exactly. Was that really possible?

One look—and the accompanying frantic thudding of her heart—and she knew her ears and brain were working just fine. Because it was *him.*

"Oh, my God," he whispered, shocked, frozen, staring as thoroughly as she was. "Lucy?"

She nodded slowly, not taking her eyes off him, wondering why the years had made him even more attractive than ever. It didn't seem fair. Not when she'd spent the past six years thinking he must have started losing that thick, golden-brown hair, or added a spare tire to that trim, muscular form.

No.

The man was gorgeous. Truly, without-a-doubt, mouth-wateringly handsome, every bit as hot as he'd been the first time she'd laid eyes on him. She'd been twenty-two, he one year older.

They'd shared an amazing holiday season.

And had never seen one another again.

Until now.

Find out what happens in
IT HAPPENED ONE CHRISTMAS
by Leslie Kelly.
Available December 2011, only from Harlequin® Blaze™

LAURA MARIE ALTOM
brings you
another touching tale from

When family tragedy forces Wyatt Buckhorn to pair up
with his longtime secret crush, Natalie Poole, and care
for the Buckhorn clan's seven children, Wyatt worries
he's in over his head. Fearing his shameful secret will
be exposed, Wyatt tries to fight his growing attraction
to Natalie. As Natalie begins to open up to Wyatt,
he starts yearning for a family of his own—a family
with Natalie. But can Wyatt trust his heart enough
to reveal his secret?

A Baby in His Stocking

Available December
wherever books are sold!

www.Harlequin.com

HAR75387

Harlequin Romance

SUSAN MEIER

*Experience the thrill of falling in love
this holiday season with*

Kisses on Her Christmas List

When Shannon Raleigh saw Rory Wallace staring at her
across her family's department store, she knew he would
be trouble…for her heart. Guarded, but unable to fight
her attraction, Shannon is drawn to Rory and his inquisitive
daughter. Now with only seven days to convince this
straitlaced businessman that what they feel for each other
is real, Shannon hopes for a Christmas miracle.

**Will the magic of Christmas be enough
to melt his heart?**

Available December 6, 2011.

Snowflake Bride

JILLIAN HART

Grateful when she is hired as a maid, Ruby Ballard vows to use her wages to save her family's farm. But the boss's son, Lorenzo, is entranced by this quiet beauty. He knows Ruby is the only woman he could marry, yet she refuses his courtship. As the holidays approach, he is determined to win her affections and make her his snowflake bride.

Available November 2011
wherever books are sold.

www.LoveInspiredBooks.com

LIH82891R